Calm Before the Storm

Calm Before the *Storm*

A NOVEL BY

Catherine Coffey

Calm Before the Storm is a work of fiction.
Names, characters, places and incidents are the products of the author's imagination or are used fictitiously. Any resemblance to actual events, locales, or persons, living or dead, is entirely coincidental.

Copyright © 2018 by Catherine Coffey
All rights reserved. No part of this book may be used or reproduced in any form, electronic or mechanical, including photocopying, recording, or scanning into any information storage and retrieval system, without written permission from the author except in the case of brief quotation embodied in critical articles and reviews.

Front and Back Cover: Original paintings by Maria Teresa Figliomeni
www.mariateresafigliomeni.com

Book design by The Troy Book Makers

Printed in the United States of America

The Troy Book Makers • Troy, New York • thetroybookmakers.com

To order additional copies of this title, contact your favorite local bookstore or visit www.shoptbmbooks.com

ISBN: 978-1-61468-446-6

Acknowledgements

I owe a tremendous debt of gratitude to the Rudy Stempel Family Sawmill in East Berne, New York. A sincere and heartfelt thank you to Brian and Sandra Stempel for sharing their knowledge, passion and legacy of the running of a sawmill and the fine art of harvesting trees.

An affectionate thank you to my friend Laurie Collins of Rensselaer, New York - she is the finest quilt maker I've ever known.

Also by Catherine Coffey

SECOND CHANCE AT SUNRISE

Mystery, danger, and love await Ashleigh Grant as she relocates to London, England to start again after the tragic loss of her family. Her best friend has offered her a job and a place to live. As soon as Ashleigh arrives in London, she starts to discover that people and places aren't what they seem to be. She becomes embroiled in a mystery that spans several continents and along the way she makes some unexpected allies. Ashleigh follows her heart in a determined effort to manage all that is being thrown her way. Her journey pushes her to new heights and affords her a second chance at happiness.

For Peter

CHAPTER
One

I was almost certain that I had been born in the wrong century and in the wrong country. Of this I had been convinced, probably due to the very mystery of my being. More than likely I belonged in Europe to some royal family or at least I liked to fantasize it was that way. But who was I? Where did I belong? What was the truth about my origin? Although I did my best to suppress them, these questions did continue to plague my daily existence, which had been one of just trying to survive one day at a time. In addition to basic survival it seemed I spent month after month and year after year trying to make something of myself, but always with what I perceived as the same result – failure.

At least that was my interpretation of the dozens of jobs I'd had, no life-long friends to speak of, no family and no sense of direction or purpose. Perhaps I should have been able to overcome or perhaps it should have made no difference at all, but I had come to believe that the very mystery of my existence was at the root of my perpetual state of insecurity, lack of confidence, sense of uneasiness and subsequently, my failure to become....whatever it was that I was supposed to be.

For years life had been moving along mostly monotonously, like a rote rehearsal for a play performed a thousand times. I got up, I went to work at this job and that, I came home, I barely socialized and I always took extra work just to pay the bills. This was it, day in and year out. And despite this pathetic routine, there was frequently something stirring deep within me, an unrest and a feeling that something was incomplete, that something was going to happen – a kind of calm before the storm. I couldn't put my finger on what it was and I didn't know when or if it would happen. But at some point every morning, I would find myself wondering if this day might be 'the day.'

I was anxious and apprehensively mulling all this over in my mind while sitting in the lavish reception room of one of the city's leading law firms, and I hadn't the slightest idea why I was there. I had been summoned there by letter – the honor of my presence being requested on such and such a date and time, so on and so forth.

It did cross my mind that perhaps my past had caught up with me. I was an orphan and a runaway, at that. No, runaway was not correct, as I had been sixteen when I had taken leave of institutional life. I had been passed from family to family, some good and some not so good. I had never really bonded with any of the families, although there were people who really treated me as one of their own. But for me there was always the feeling of incompleteness and then, back to the orphanage. It seemed to be inevitable no matter how hard I tried to fit in.

And so at sixteen, I struck out on my own determined to make myself complete or let fate have its way with me. I was now grown up and long past the age for which the state would care about my well-being and I had pretty much stuck to the straight and narrow path in life so, rack my brain as I might, I could not really account for my invitation to visit the prestigious law firm. My thoughts were interrupted as a woman called my name.

"Holly Snow," she said.

I rose from my chair and followed her down a long corridor that had doors on both sides. Eventually she opened a door then stood aside, motioning for me to enter a large room.

"Please take a seat Miss Snow. They'll be with you shortly," she directed.

I did what she commanded, seating myself at the large table in a chair that faced the door. In an effort to control my anxiety, I began to study the room. The walls were decorated with ornate moldings and portraits of official looking men, probably previous partners of the firm, and no doubt some of whom were still practicing. The room was an interior one and therefore had no access to daylight, consequently creating a somewhat stuffy and stifling atmosphere.

At one end of the room a slide projector stood silent but ready to relay images onto a screen on the other end of the room that hung from the ceiling. In one corner, of all things, stood a bar. It hardly seemed the sort of place one would be having a cocktail, although

I supposed that joyful transactions took place in the room as well as painful ones. I wondered which kind mine would be. This time my thoughts were interrupted as the door opened to admit two well-dressed, middle-aged gentlemen. I rose to greet them.

"Miss Snow, I am Gerard Manning and this is my associate Michael Bell." I shook hands across the table with each man. "Please take your seat," the man continued as he and his colleague seated themselves across the table from me.

"Have you any idea why you have been called here?" he asked.

"No sir," I replied.

Mr. Bell spoke up, "Mr. Manning and I represent your parents."

I was shocked and confused. "My parents?" I echoed. "I am an orphan," I said somewhat naively.

"It is more accurate to say that we represent your parents' estates," said Mr. Manning offering clarification. "I have the very sad duty of informing you that your father has recently passed away. Your mother died five years ago."

I sat immobilized, hardly breathing. Obviously I had parents. As a child I fantasized about them. As a teenager I denied their existence and as an adult I found myself plagued by the feelings of incompleteness that had fueled the curiosity about who I was, leaving me with a strong hope that I might one day find out. Now all feelings – hopes, fears and angers – had been suddenly yanked away leaving in their place a cold numbness and a growing nausea.

"We realize this news is a shock to you Miss Snow," continued Mr. Bell, "however, we have a great deal of information to share with you. This must be done now as you will be required to be present at the reading of your father's will next week."

I must have looked positively ill. Mr. Manning pressed a button on the phone that was sitting on the table and asked for water to be brought in.

"My dear," he said, "can you manage to continue?"

"How did you find me?" I blurted out. "How do you know I am the person you are looking for?"

Within seconds the woman who had ushered me into the room entered carrying a tray containing a pitcher of water and glasses. She set it on the table near me, glancing at me, and then at the men, but saying nothing as she quietly retreated. I poured myself a drink. Mr. Manning had risen and was making his way to the slide projector, dimming the lights as he went.
He turned on the machine and at once the picture of a woman flashed onto the screen. It was like looking at myself in the mirror.

"Samantha Moorehead, your mother," he started, "seen here at about age forty. Youngest child and only daughter of Edgar and Alicia Moorehead. Family of seamen with a proud tradition dating back to the early settling of the colonies. Your grandfather was a sea captain who, mid career, turned to tending the light at Henderson Point, Maine. That is where your mother spent all of her life. In fact, she took over her father's job of tending the light upon his death and worked at the lighthouse until her own death five years ago."

I could hardly take my eyes from her picture. I felt such joy at seeing her face and such intense sorrow at knowing that I would never hear her voice or hold her close. My mind was reeling with questions but I was unable to speak. With the click of a button, the image on the screen changed. I was now looking at a split screen – a younger and an older version – of the man I presumed was my father.

"Nicholas Xavier Rothchilde, your father," continued the attorney, "only child and heir to a vast fortune made in the shipping and railroad industries. Survived by his wife and only son, and of course, you. Your father and mother met one summer while his family was vacationing in Maine. They fell in love but he was already married and managing his family's companies. He purchased a lumber milling operation in a town not far from your mother's so he could continue to see her regularly. Your mother, being unmarried and with limited finances, traveled out of state and gave birth and then turned you over to an orphanage at the urging of her parents. She did not tell your father about you until many, many years later."

"My name is Snow," I protested.

Mr. Bell spoke up. "Winter was your mother's favorite time of year. When you were born 'Holly Snow' was the name she gave on your birth certificate."

"How do you know….." I started.

Again Mr. Bell interrupted. "I have been your mother's attorney for the past twenty years and as such have been privy to the details, many intimate, of her life."

"Why now?" I asked. "Why not before she died? Why not after she told him about me? Why did they leave me alone for so long?"

"Your mother spent most of her life anguishing over the decision she had made," the lawyer answered. "She believed it best to give you up as she had no spouse, limited education and little money. It was her hope that you had been adopted by a loving family and had been given all that she felt she could not give you herself. It was not until the later years of her life that she sought you out and learned that you had remained under the care of the orphanage until your sixteenth year, since placement hadn't worked out."

"We searched for you for years and were finally able to discover that you were living and working here in New York," he continued. "The search was long and difficult, what with little to go on once you left the orphanage. The countless interviews and man-hours spent looking and verifying and pouring over false leads. Our big break came five years ago when you took your current job. You routinely messenger documents to the courthouse and as you…."

"My fingerprints!" I interrupted.

"Yes," he said, "they are kept on file and as your mother's investigator periodically checked the database for updates it was only a matter of time. Your mother had decided to contact you but she died before that could happen."

"How did she die?" I asked.

"She was killed in a car accident," he answered.

"And my father?" I demanded. "What of him? How long has he known about me?"

"Your father and mother remained extremely close all the years of their lives. She told him about you only months before her death," replied Mr. Manning.

"So, you are saying that he knew about me for the last five years but made no attempt to contact me?"

"That is correct," said Mr. Manning. "He has been watching and waiting."

"Watching and waiting!" I repeated angrily. "Look, just what is it you people want?"

Mr. Bell said calmly, "My dear, I can only imagine how upsetting this must be for you, to be called into the office of complete strangers and told your life story in such an impersonal way. I am certain that you have many questions, some of which I know we can help you answer. Please let me assure you that we are here to assist you. Perhaps a sip of water..."

Obligingly, I took a sip.

"It was your mother's wish that you should inherit the lighthouse at Henderson Point," he continued. "Your father eventually purchased the land and the light from the coast guard and gave it to her, as the property held such great sentimental value for her. She wanted you to have it, along with the truth about her, on your twenty-fifth birthday, which, I believe, is later this month. Your father was aware of her wish and was watching and waiting for the time when all would be revealed. It was then that he intended to make himself known to you. However, his untimely death..."

"Untimely death?" I cut in.

"He was killed in an automobile accident," stated Mr. Manning.

"Didn't you say that's how my mother died?" I asked.

"Yes," said Mr. Manning, "strange coincidence that."

There was something about the way in which he made the comment that caught my attention. I had no chance to question him, however, as Mr. Bell was carrying on.

"Now, your father has left you the lump sum of one million dollars cash and you are to receive a monthly allowance from the lumber company in Maine, er, that is accurate is it not, Gerard?" he asked his colleague, but he continued on, not waiting for a response. "The mill will remain a Rothchilde subsidiary but you will be owner and manager. We can make arrangements for your name to be changed and for you to have an advance on your inheritance if you should need it. You will need to be present at the reading of the will to be held at this office in exactly six days. You may wish to have your own attorney present."

My head was throbbing but I managed to ask, "My own attorney?"

"Yes, my dear," said Mr. Manning, "technically we work for your parents and their estates. It would be wise to have your own legal advisor present."

I rose. Suddenly I felt an overwhelming desire for a breath of fresh air.

"May I go?" I inquired.

"But…" started Mr. Bell.

"There is nothing I want from you today," I said. "I'm sure you can understand that my life has been turned upside down. I need to…I would like some time to myself."

The two men looked at each other and then at me. Neither spoke.

"I will come back for the reading of the will," I promised.

This seemed to satisfy them. Mr. Manning shut off the projector and crossed the room silently. He took a business card from his shirt pocket, turned it over and quickly wrote something on it. He handed it to me as he opened the door. I took it, walked out and did not look back.

Outside the legal office, I impatiently paced up and down the hall waiting for the elevator with the words I had just heard playing over and over in my head – my parents, one million dollars, a lighthouse, a lumber mill, car accidents. I looked at the business card clutched in my hand. The day and time of the reading of the will was written there. I opened my handbag and deposited the card into it.

I pushed the elevator's call button again and again and finally headed for the stairwell. The law office was on the seventeenth floor. I started my descent walking, but the more I contemplated what I had just heard the faster my pace became. I ended up running, taking two steps at a time, down to the first floor and out the door where I leaned against the building, gasping for air, heart pounding. I was so overwrought I could barely think.

Dazed and without purpose I eventually started walking and found myself standing with a group of people waiting to cross the street. Suddenly I felt a blow to my back. I pitched forward and fell into the street, hitting my head on the pavement. As I struggled to sit up I could hear people gasping and screaming. All at once I saw the grill of an oncoming taxicab approaching fast. I could hear the horn blowing but in my stupor I was slow to react. A man came dashing into the street from out of the crowd. With one hand under my arm and the other on my shirt collar he dragged me the rest of the way across the street to safety.

I could hear cheers of relief and thunderous applause from the crowd that had witnessed the event. My savior said nothing but held me in his arms like a limp rag doll. I remember thinking that he had the kindest eyes I'd ever seen, and somehow, he seemed vaguely familiar.

"You have the kindest eyes I've ever seen," I told him, before I passed out in his arms.

When I came to, I was sitting, propped up against a wall. Several policemen were standing around me and a small group of on-lookers was hovering close by. Immediately I became aware of a fierce and throbbing pain between my shoulder blades that ran up my neck and into my head.

"Well now young lady," said one of the officers, "can you tell us what happened?" he asked, as he bent down next to me and opened his notebook, preparing to take down my statement.

I remembered the visit to the lawyer, finding out about my parents, leaving the office and walking to the corner…I was pushed, it suddenly occurred to me. Aloud I said, "I was standing with a group of people waiting to cross when I was pushed into the street."

"Pushed?" the man repeated. "Are you certain? Did you see someone? Can you identify who might have done such a thing?"

"Unfortunately not. But as I think back, I am certain I was shoved," I answered. "It's possible someone standing in the group saw something. Have you…"

"Been interviewing the onlookers but with no luck. Only person they saw was your rescuer," he replied.

That reminded me of the man who had saved my life. I would never forget his face. I scanned the crowd hoping to catch a glimpse of him.

The officer noticed my inquiring glance and said, "Once he saw you were safe, he called for us and left the scene. Any idea who he was?"

"I never saw him before," I answered. But I did recall the feeling that he had seemed somehow familiar to me. I tried to put a name with the face but couldn't, probably due to the tremendous pain in my head.

"Well, lucky for you he happened along when he did. Now then, we'll just take a few more details for the paperwork and then we'll be happy to give you a lift home, or to the hospital if you think that bump on your head needs attention."

We finished the paperwork and I gratefully accepted a ride home.

CHAPTER
Two

Six days later saw me back in the waiting area of the posh law firm. This time, however, I was not alone. I had been working for the last five years as an assistant to a somewhat well known attorney who mostly handled divorce cases, which accounted for my frequent visits to the courthouse. I had confided in him about my fantastic trip to the law firm, giving him the basic details. He knew nothing about estate law but as he liked me well enough, he'd agreed to come along and see that everything appeared to be on the up and up. We were escorted toward the conference room I had previously visited and as we approached, the sound of voices, loud and argumentative, reached our ears.

"What is her background? What training has she had in this type of industry? I won't allow that company to be run by a homeless, uneducated girl…" It had been a woman doing the talking and she was interrupted by a male voice.

"Mother, please, that will do. She will be here any moment."

The secretary, looking slightly embarrassed about the fact that we had overheard the exchange, pushed the door open all the way and announced us. I recognized Mr. Bell and Mr. Manning and I presumed I was now looking at Mrs. Rothchilde and my half brother. As I stood there staring at them, the two attorneys rose to greet us.

"My dear, so good to see you again," said Mr. Bell, "and you have brought counsel?"

"Yes," I answered, finding my voice. "May I introduce William Kincade." The men shook hands.

"And may I present Margaret and Maxmillian Rothchilde," continued Mr. Bell. Neither mother nor son acknowledged the introduction and, following their lead, William and I remained silent as we took our seats. Mr. Bell said, "Well, then, as we're all assembled, let us begin."

The attorneys launched into the lengthy disposition of Nicholas Xavier Rothchilde's property. In short, everything had been left to his wife and son, with the exception of the sawmill in Maine and the sum of one million dollars cash, which had been left to yours truly. I could feel Mrs. Rothchilde's cold stare of hatred upon me, and I knew she begrudged me even such a small share of her husband's vast estate. After all, I was the product of his love for, and secret life with, another woman. Obviously that very fact alone was enough to make her despise me.

My brother said nothing throughout the entire proceeding. He sat perfectly poised, occasionally patting his mother's hand. He didn't look at me but I found myself stealing glances at him, trying to sense some level of connection, although there was none. My head ached fiercely.

Just when I thought I could bear no more, Mr. Manning announced the proceedings concluded. Without a word, Margaret Rothchilde got up and left the room. Maxmillian turned to me.

"I am so very sorry that your introduction to the family has had to be under such difficult circumstances," he said apologetically. "Please forgive mother. This has been extremely hard for her. If you need anything, here is my card. I hope that we can talk soon. You can reach me at the number listed there."

"Thank you," I said, taking the card. He had been very kind under the circumstances, I thought, and I felt that I should say something more, but I didn't know what that was. I merely stood there staring at him. He turned and left the room.

"Are you alright my dear?" asked Mr. Manning.

"Oh, yes," I replied, although that couldn't have been farther from the truth. "Which of us is older?" I asked suddenly.

"You are the eldest child," he answered handing me an envelope. "You will find contained therein the sum of three thousand dollars cash, directions to Henderson Point, keys to the lighthouse and a list of relatives from both sides that you may wish to contact when you feel ready. We will forward copies of today's paperwork to you at the lighthouse. For years after your mother's death an elderly neighbor kept up the grounds. However, he passed away about a year ago so you are likely to find the grounds quite overgrown."

"Now," added Mr. Bell, "once you are settled, we will arrange a wire transfer of your money into the bank of your choice. You will receive a check monthly via the United States mail from the mill. As for your name, do you wish us to file the necessary paperwork to change it over?"

I stood silently thinking about what he had asked. "May I let you know about that at a later date?" I inquired. "I have no idea who I am."

The men looked at each other and then at me, nodding their heads. After signing paperwork, William and I prepared to leave.

"We will be in touch soon," said Mr. Manning. "Please feel free to contact me, should you need anything." The way he spoke to me and looked at me made me feel as if he were trying to communicate some silent message to me, but I couldn't imagine what that might be.

"Yes, I will and thank you," I said.

William offered his arm as we left the office. I readily accepted it and clung to it for support.

CHAPTER
Three

Those deep waters of incompleteness, which had remained still, were definitely swirling and I now knew that I had just barely scratched the surface of my book of revelations. None of it made any sense yet, but I knew that my day had finally arrived. In a way, I was excited but at the same time, scared as hell, and hoping that the long and difficult journey on which I was about to embark would, for once and for all, provide the inner peace that I was so desperately longing for.

I had quit my job, thanking William profusely for all he had done for me, packed what few earthly possessions I owned into my car and bade goodbye to my roommates. The reading of the will had taken place on a sunny Monday afternoon in mid-September. Thursday morning just after dawn, I started out hoping that my old car could make the approximately twelve-hour journey to my new home.

I made my way north, stopping every couple of hours for a break, which the car needed as much as I did. Eventually I connected with I-95 and then turned off onto Route 27, which I was to follow until it dead-ended on Henderson Point. The Point, according to the map, lay between Boothbay Harbor and Pemaquid Point.

I drove through what could definitely be described as small, picture-perfect New England-like towns and I enjoyed soaking in the charm of it all. It felt like I was driving to the ends of the Earth when I finally saw a sign that said, 'Henderson Point, 2 miles'. When I finally reached the town, it was as enchanting as those I had already passed. I drove slowly trying to make mental notes of where I could purchase groceries and gasoline.

I saw another sign that said, 'Henderson Point Lighthouse, 1 mile' with an arrow indicating the direction. I continued straight on the main road all the way through town and beyond. The main road ended by forming a perpendicular design. It ended at a stop sign. The driver could make a left or a right turn to continue driving. But across the street from the stop sign, I saw a dirt driveway with a mailbox at the edge of the pavement. I moved the car across the road and stopped to examine it. The name 'Moorehead' appeared on the box in faded black letters. The house wouldn't be far.

I moved the car ahead slowly. The driveway was surrounded on each side by a dense forest of pine, maple, oak and birch trees. The maple and oak trees were almost at the peak of their color change. The driveway was long and narrow but all at once it spilled out onto the point. Just beyond the trees I saw it, and the sight of it sent waves of anticipation and apprehension through me. I stopped the car and got out, shutting the door behind me.

Sitting proudly on the point, near the edge of a cliff, was the house, and just behind it, the light. The house was an L-shaped Cape Cod style made from bricks that had been painted white. The roof was red slate and rising up out of it in three locations were chimneys, also brick painted white. The front of the house featured two oversized, multi-paned windows. The second floor sported dormer windows and some small, four-paned windows, these mostly framing the chimneys. The light tower mimicked the main house – brick, painted white with a red slate cap.

There were several maple trees next to the house. A white picket fence edged a stone path that lead to the front door, which was painted red. One had to pass beneath a white, vine-covered trellis to reach the door. The place looked like it belonged on a postcard and the grounds were perfectly manicured. I recalled that Mr. Manning had said I was likely to find the yard overgrown. Yet, the place certainly did not give the appearance of having been deserted for years. I wondered who could have readied it for my arrival. I wondered who knew I was coming.

As I stood there taking it all in, I heard the sound of a car approaching. As it came closer I could see that it was a sort of small delivery truck.

"Afternoon!" called a man from behind the wheel. "You must be Miss Snow."

"Yes, I am," I answered.

"Welcome. Name's Horace Cunningham. The wife and I run a small market about a mile back. We opened in 1960 and have been runnin' it for thirty-five years. Brought your groceries. Be glad to help you inside with 'em."

His warm welcome made me smile and I was certainly glad to see a friendly face. But I was bewildered as to who had placed the order. It certainly hadn't been me.

"Mr. Cunningham, I didn't order any food. Are you certain you have the correct address?" I asked.

"Oh yes, ma'am," he said smiling as he climbed out of the automobile. "Been delivering to the Mooreheads for decades. Order was placed by a friend."

"This friend didn't happen to leave a name?" I inquired.

"Funny that," he continued, "said it was to be a surprise for you. Can tell you it was a man."

I thought possibly it may have been Maxmillian trying to make a gesture of kindness. Or perhaps Mr. Manning. He had certainly been making every effort to help me through my life-altering experience. My new neighbor had moved to the rear of his vehicle and was collecting the bags. He was an older man with graying hair, average height and still strong. He picked up the bags, stacking them two on each arm, like they were light as feathers.

"You lead, I'll follow," he suggested.

In a way his timing couldn't have been better. I was grateful to have somebody with me as I entered the house for the first time. He followed me up the path, under the trellis and toward the front door. I opened the screen door and then tried inserting several keys into the front door lock before finding the correct one. I took a deep breath as I opened the door and we stepped inside into a lovely foyer with a stone floor, bench seats, hangers on the wall for coats and mats ready to hold muddy boots. Mr. Cunningham offered to take the groceries through to the kitchen. I moved into the living room and stood silently, surveying the room.

It was as if time had stood still. The rooms I could see were completely furnished with pieces from the eighteen and nineteen-hundreds, I guessed, and everything stood in its place as if the family would be returning at any moment. There were magazines on the coffee table and a bowl of fresh fruit. Obviously that hadn't been there for five years. A quilt rested on the arm of a rocking chair that was placed quite close to the fireplace. At the foot of the rocker stood a basket full of wood for the fire.

The mantelpiece was crowded with framed photographs – males, females, young, old and group pictures – all freshly dusted. I realized suddenly that the odor penetrating my nostrils was not the musty one I had expected, but rather the pleasant smell of cleaning fluids. Someone had certainly gone to great lengths to prepare for my arrival.

A tremendous wave of emotion overtook me. My people, my family had lived here, loved here, died here. There was too much commotion in my mind as if the ghosts of the past were trying to rush in. I felt an overwhelming need for air and raced out the front door.

"Miss Snow, you alright?" Mr. Cunningham asked, following me outdoors.

"Oh yes. I…it's all just a bit much and I've a terrible headache, probably from the long drive," I answered. "I'll be fine. Mr. Cunningham, do you happen to know which key belongs to the light tower?" I asked, showing him my key ring.

"It's this one, here," he said, holding up the metal instrument for me to see. "Light's on an automatic timer now what with no one tending to it and there is a backup generator. Nothing you need do right away. And please, ma'am, call me Horace."

"Thank you, Horace," I said. "By the way, how do I get into the tower?"

"Out the kitchen door and follow the path. Leads you right to the door," he answered. "Left my telephone number on the kitchen counter if you should be needing anything. Please call, we are open every day. You be alright?" he inquired eyeing me intensely.

"Oh, yes," I said trying to convince him, as well as myself. "Thank you, you've been very kind. I will come and visit you at your store soon." Seeming satisfied that I could be left by myself, he walked back to his truck and drove off with a wave of his hand.

I looked at the house. I slowly headed toward the front door again, realizing that this was going to be much harder than I had imagined it would be. In one way, I felt like an intruder and in another, I felt the vaguest sense of belonging. I had been on a lifelong quest to belong somewhere and to someone, and now that a family had been handed to me, and on a silver platter, it was as if I couldn't cope.

I had another raging headache, which wasn't helping matters. I had never been particularly prone to having headaches and suddenly I couldn't go a day without one. As I neared the house I could hear the telephone ringing. I hurried through the front door and then stopped in my tracks realizing that I didn't know where the device was located. I made a quick visual sweep of the living room and the study next to it and came up empty. I continued on to the kitchen. The phone was hanging on the wall next to the door.

"Hello?" I said breathlessly.

"Hello, Holly? This is Max, your…brother. Have I caught you at a bad time?"

"I…no…I couldn't find the telephone," I answered, reflecting on his choice of words. After all, he was indeed family. "How are you?" I asked trying to think of what to say.

"Very well, thank you. I called to see that you arrived safely and ask if there is anything I can do, or anything that you need?" he said.

"That is very thoughtful of you," I replied, realizing from his offer that it was probably not he who had sent the groceries. "How did you know I'd be here?"

"I phoned Mr. Manning and asked how I could get in touch with you," he explained. "He advised me that you should be arriving there sometime today. I hope that it wasn't too forward of me to call."

"Oh, no, of course not," I said. "The trip was long and I am tired, but at the moment I am set, thank you."

"You have my number should you need me. I tell you what, I am going to call tomorrow after you've had a chance to rest and settle in. We'll chat then," he said.

"That sounds fine," I said.

"Goodbye for now," he said and rang off.

I stood there trying to grasp the concept that I had just had a conversation with my brother. The word brother had such a nice sound. I wondered if I would ever really come to know him as a brother in the true sense of the word. I hoped so and was glad that he was attempting to reach out. It was obvious that his mother wanted nothing to do with me and would probably be urging him to avoid me altogether.

My head was still pounding and I went out to the car to get an aspirin from my handbag. I made a couple of trips back and forth from the car to the house, bringing in some of my suitcases. I guessed there were only a couple of hours of daylight left and decided that the rest of my belongings could wait until morning.

Back inside, I decided to take a quick tour of the house and get my bearings. Then after a quick bite to eat, I was going to retire for the evening. The living room and the study opposite it both had fireplaces. The study had a massive, wooden roll-top desk positioned quite close to the fireplace. The fireplace was made of pieces of stone that went from floor to ceiling. The mantel was made of a beautiful piece of wood, with bark left on the edging and the hearth was made from one huge, thick piece of stone. I noted that the living room's fireplace was a twin to this one.

Above the fireplace mantel in the study hung a huge portrait of a sea captain. I assumed the man in the picture to be my grandfather, but as I moved closer to study the name plate on the bottom of the frame, I saw the name Peter Joseph Moorehead written there. The man looking back at me was older with a beautifully groomed white wavy beard and sideburns. He had a very tan, weather-worn face. His eyes were full of knowledge and experience, but they were warm and kind and were framed by bushy white eyebrows. He was wearing a yellow sweater covered by a large bulky wool jacket and he was wearing his sea captain's hat. The artist had certainly captured a life-like essence.

Flanking the fireplace on each side stood bookshelves, still completely stocked. One thing I had been for as far back as I could remember was an avid reader. Reading had been a source of countless hours of entertainment, education and even escapism for me.

I made a mental note to set aside time over the next several days to discover just what types of books the cases held. Not only would the books serve as a source of entertainment, but they might also provide some insight on my family members. Above each bookshelf was a small, four-paned window from which I could view the ocean.

Across the room from the desk and standing next to a window was a grandfather clock – one that reached from the floor almost to the room's ceiling. It was working, and I wondered if it could possibly have run by itself, without human assistance, for five years. One of the room's most interesting features was its pocket doors – paneled, wooden doors that slid effortlessly into a narrow opening in the wall so as to be hidden from view. Yet when the study's occupant wanted privacy, the doors could easily be retrieved from their holding place.

Another striking feature about the study, and the living room, was that the walls had been painted a subtle shade of taupe and the trim – moldings, windows, doors - had been stained a rich maple color. The combination of the subtle paint and the richly stained wood was visually stunning and left one feeling warm and welcome.

I left the study passing back through the living room and on into the kitchen. This was a large room, painted yellow with maple-stained moldings, cabinets and doors, and a place where the family probably spent much of their time. The flooring was made from wide planked wood, just as it had been in the two front rooms. Almost centered in the room was a big rectangular table around which stood six chairs.

The table was made of wood that had been painted white, which over the years, probably due to use, had developed a distressed look about it. It gave a rustic yet comfortable feeling to the room.

There was a large cast iron gas stove along one wall. The body was black and the doors were white with brushed silver handles. There were six burners and two oven doors with doors on the side and above for storage. I wondered if I could ever learn how to use it. The refrigerator was a small stainless steel colored appliance and the large farm sink was white with a brushed silver faucet and handles.

I stole a quick glance out the back door, which I suddenly noticed was strategically placed directly opposite the front door. The deliberate positioning of the doors must have allowed for an excellent cross breeze on hot summer days. I saw the stone path Horace had mentioned but I decided to leave a detailed exploration of the back yard and the light tower until morning.

Opposite the kitchen was a formal dining room, which along with the family room beyond it, made up the longest portion of the 'L' shape of the house. The dining room featured a large wooden table with eight chairs. An enormous sideboard on the wall was placed just beneath a large multi-paned window that looked out over the ocean. The family room contained many cozy looking chairs, a large coffee table and a television. It also featured a stone fireplace, larger than the ones in the living room and study. I imagined that this room must have been a favorite one for the family to gather in.

I retraced my steps back to the kitchen and climbed the staircase located there. It was steep and narrow and led up to a long hallway. I made a right turn at the top of the stairs and followed the hall toward the front of the house. The wooden floorboards creaked beneath my feet. At the end of the hall there was a bedroom on either side and each had its own fireplace. I headed back toward the stairs, across from which was the bathroom. At the other end of the hall, at the rear of the house closest to the tower, there were bedrooms again on either side of the hall.

All of the bedrooms were about the same size, but for some reason I decided I would occupy one of the rooms in the front of the house, the one above the study. The bedrooms, just like the rooms below, stood fully furnished. I went back to the room I had chosen. The room had two large dormer windows – one overlooking the front yard and one, to my delight, overlooking the ocean. The fireplace stood on the same wall as the dormer window with the ocean view, although the two were some distance from each other with the fireplace being closer to the front corner of the room.

A canopy bed stood atop a worn, multi-colored braided area rug, which in turn covered only a small portion of the wooden floor. I drew the conclusion that the room had belonged to a girl due to the pale pink walls, a number of dolls scattered about, the frilly bedcover with matching canopy, and the nic nacs laying about the dresser, and this could mean only one thing. There was a desk under the front window and as I drew closer to it looking for confirmation of the room's previous occupant, I could see boxes of stationary and a small address book. I opened its cover and printed neatly inside was the name Samantha Moorehead.

The room had indeed belonged to my mother. Inexplicably or maybe completely understandably,

I began to cry. In my mind I put it down to being exhausted from the trip and the stress of the last week. But in my heart I knew it was due to the bittersweet happiness of having at long last come home.

I hastened downstairs to lock up and get my bags. I was too tired to eat. I left a light on in the living room and one on in the kitchen, as I didn't want to come downstairs to a dark and unfamiliar house if I woke during the night and then climbed the stairs once again. I didn't bother to change my clothes. I curled up on my mother's bed and fell asleep.

CHAPTER
Four

Holly.

I tossed and turned.

Holly, can you hear me?

I opened my eyes and looked around. I was disoriented but quickly remembered that I had made it to the lighthouse. I could see that it was still dark outside.

Holly.

It was then that I realized that someone was calling my name. I reached out, groping for the lamp next to the bed and almost knocking it off the nightstand. I switched it on.

Holly, can you hear me?

There was no one in the room except myself but I was not mistaken about the fact that I was hearing voices.

"Who's there?" I called out.

There was no answer. I cautiously slipped out of bed and went to the doorway. I peered across the hall into the neighboring bedroom and then down the hall. I could see no one. My head was pounding again and I remembered I had left my handbag on the kitchen counter. I cautiously made my way to the stairs and slowly descended into the kitchen. The house stood quiet. I took another aspirin and, as I prepared to climb the stairs, I heard it again.

Holly...

My head was throbbing. I managed to make it up the stairs and back into bed before passing out.

I awoke to the sound of the telephone ringing, and I didn't have to look far for it as it was on the nightstand next to the bed.

"Hello?" I said.

"Miss Snow? It's Mr. Manning. I am sorry, did I wake you?" he asked.

"No...yes...I didn't sleep very well," I managed.

"First night in a new place and all that, I imagine," he said.

"Yes... oh, thank you for the groceries," I said, struggling to sit up and hang on to the receiver at the same time.

"Groceries? Actually I was phoning to see that you arrived safely and if you needed anything," he replied.

"So far, so good," I answered, realizing that he had not been the one who sent the supplies. What other male friend did I have, I wondered?

"I will be in Henderson Point on Monday and I would like to stop by to see you," he was saying. "I thought we could take care of some of your banking."

"That would be fine Mr. Manning, I'd really appreciate that," I answered. I'd only had a couple of encounters with the man, but he had been kind to me and I found myself comforted by the thought of his visit.

"Very well, my dear, I will see you Monday," he said, and rang off.

As soon as our connection terminated, his words sunk in and I realized that the reading of the will had happened only days ago and he was making a trip to see me already. I remembered having the feeling that there was something he wanted to tell me the day the will had been read, and I concluded that it must be important to make him come see me so soon. It would be interesting to see what Monday would bring.

I glanced at the clock on the mantel above the fireplace. Ten o'clock! I had overslept my usual wake-up call by several hours. Well after all, I thought as I forgave myself, yesterday had been quite a day. I noticed that the lamp on the nightstand was on and suddenly I remembered the voice. But I couldn't decide if there had really been a voice or if it had just been a dream.

I looked around the room. I studied every object in it as if familiarizing myself with each one would somehow make me know my mother. Tears came and I allowed myself to sink into the depths of pity and despair. It was incredibly ironic that here I was in my family's house, with no family to share it with. I forced myself to get up and change my clothes. After straightening the bed I went across the hall to examine the neighboring bedroom.

At once I knew it must have belonged to my grandparents, the people who had encouraged my mother to give me up. I definitely had conflicting feelings about them. My mother must have made her peace with them, however, because the room was nothing short of a shrine to her parents. Everything was in its proper place. A shawl was draped over the back of the chair near the fireplace and knitting needles and yarn were in the basket at the foot of the chair. Pipes of all sizes and configurations were lined up neatly on the dresser, and a glass container of tobacco stood full next to them. Near this lay a woman's comb and brush set.

The hat stand in the corner of the room held several hats, a style for practically every occasion my grandmother could have used one, and on a hanger, still neatly pressed, was a man's dress uniform. The brass double bed was meticulously made, although the spread was quite worn and at the foot of the bed stood a tray table holding a teapot, cup and linen napkin.

The room's outer wall contained a fireplace and a large dormer window and there was another dormer window overlooking the front yard just like in the room in which I was staying. These windows showcased excellent views of the maple trees closest to the house and beyond this, the mouth of the driveway. My grandparents would have been able to see all of the comings and goings on the point.

On a whim I went to the closet door and pulled it open. It was empty. I moved to the dresser and opened a drawer, also empty. I crossed the hall and checked the closet and dresser drawers in my room. Empty. I wondered what had become of the absent personal items.

I moved down the hall to check out the bathroom. It was definitely turn of the century with a few modern touches added. The centerpiece of the room was the tub – a large, white, claw-footed piece of cast iron with a cistern, hot and cold water pulls and a hand-held spray. A make-shift shower head coming out of the wall was obviously an attempt at modernization. The commode was a two-piece affair – bowl on bottom and on the wall behind and above it was a box with a pull chain.

The sink was an original pedestal type with over-sized white porcelain knobs. And the floor was made from what must have been thousands of tiny pieces of black and white ceramic tiles. There was a small window in the room, which looked out over the sea.

I continued down the hall to the back bedrooms. There was no sign of who the original occupants of the rooms had been. I surmised, however, that the rooms must have belonged to my mother's brothers. These rooms mirrored each other. There were sheer curtains on the windows, a twin bed and one large dresser. No personal items of any kind.

The room on the ocean side had a fireplace next to the window that looked out on a portion of the back yard and the light tower, while the other window looked out over the ocean. The room that looked out on the back yard was smaller. It also had a window that looked out on the side of the yard and the view was of trees and the little garden next to the house. You couldn't see the driveway from this window and it didn't have a fireplace but rather grates in the floor to allow heat from downstairs to rise and warm the room.

I decided that my investigation of the outside of the house would have to wait until I'd had something to eat. I went down to the kitchen and started unpacking the bags Horace had brought, smiling as I recalled his kindness. I had refrigerated the items that needed refrigeration before I went to bed, but I had been too tired to do any more than that. I opened this cabinet and that expecting to find them empty. Several were empty but several contained drinking glasses and plates. I quickly put away the supplies and made myself a sandwich.

I carried it and a glass of milk out the back door to a small table I had seen just beyond the kitchen window. The cast iron table sat atop a small stone patio that overlooked a now terribly empty garden. Although I was no green thumb I would have to attempt some gardening in the spring. It was a cool, sunny day with a light wind blowing. All at once it started again.

Holly...

I jumped up and looked around. There was only myself and the house and the ocean.

"What is going on?" I asked aloud. "Where are you?"

Holly...I'm nearby...

I ran into the house and slammed the door. I stood there, heart pounding, wondering who would play such a trick on me. Or was the place haunted, or was I going mad? I couldn't decide.

Soon...very soon...

To my utter dismay I realized that the voice was not outside, but rather inside my mind. And again my head ached. What was happening? I felt an overwhelming need to get away from the house. I decided to take a walk. How I ended up at Horace Cunningham's store is still a blur to me. But apparently I walked a mile and nearly collapsed in front of the store. I vaguely remember Horace sitting in a rocker on the front porch. He rose immediately upon seeing me and called to his wife. Mrs. Cunningham had insisted on calling the doctor, but somehow I convinced them that all I really needed was a ride home. Horace drove me home and reluctantly left me there after my repeated reassurances that I was fine.

I ran into the house to answer my ringing telephone but my caller gave up on me for the ringing stopped just as I reached for the receiver. I noticed the glass of milk and what was left of my sandwich still sitting on the table in the back yard. After collecting them and washing the dishes, I decided to check out the tower. My mission was halted by the sound of the telephone's bell.

"Hello?" I said into the receiver.

"Hello Holly, it's Max," he said. "I've been trying to reach you and I was just starting to get worried."

"You needn't have worried," I replied. "I've been out…doing some errands," I lied, not wanting him to know my true state of mind.

"Well, I know that you are trying to cope with a great deal so I thought I would stop in to see you, if that would be agreeable to you. I thought we could catch up and I could offer you some advice on dealing with the mill," he offered. "Father had left me in charge there these past several years. Perhaps I could see you sometime during the coming week?"

Be careful…

Oh my God, it was starting again.

"Holly? Are you still there?" Max was inquiring.

"I…yes…this week…that sounds like a good idea Max," I managed.

Must take care…

"All right then," Max continued, "I'll phone you on Monday and we can make arrangements."

"Thank you Max," I said and hung up.

"Stop it!" I cried out. "Just stop it!"

Holly…

"No…. no more…" I said crying. I ran to the front door, flung it open and started toward my car. I hadn't gotten farther than just past the trellis when I realized

I'd forgotten my keys. I reluctantly stopped and turned around. I felt weak as I walked back toward the house. Instead of going in, I walked past the house, toward the edge of the cliff.

At that moment I was convinced I could not handle the new life that had been thrust upon me. I was utterly alone, scared, unsure of who I was and tormented by the voice in my head. I stood near the edge thinking how peaceful the water looked and how peaceful I would be if I only took a few steps….

"No!" said a voice loudly and authoritatively. This time, however, it was not in my head. It belonged to the man with the kind eyes, my rescuer from the street corner in New York. He was standing beside me and drawing me into his arms.

"You…it's you…." I said, sobbing as I collapsed against him.

CHAPTER

Five

The name popped into my mind. *Nicholas*. I must have started saying it out loud.

"Yes. I'm here. I'm right here." As the voice answered I felt something warm and moist touch my hand.

I opened my eyes to find a very handsome and very well-groomed golden retriever sitting next to the bed, nudging my hand. My rescuer was sitting on the edge of the bed near my feet.

"Nicholas," I said sure about the name and looking up at him. "Now I see it! You must be….we must be…."

"Yes, we are and please call me Nick," he answered smiling. "I have always looked more like your side of the family than my own. And this is Casey," he said patting the dog who was looking eagerly from one of us to the other. "Well, we had better get you something to eat," Nicholas continued. He got up and retrieved my sweater from the chair.

"It was you," I guessed suddenly. "You sent the groceries. And you've been keeping the place up."

"Yes," he acknowledged. "It was me."

I sat up and could see that night had fallen.

"You have been asleep all day - you needed the rest. Let me help you," he said offering his hand.

I looked at him. For a moment I wondered if I should be afraid. I was alone in the house with a stranger, but somehow he wasn't really a stranger, and for some reason I wasn't the least bit afraid. After all, he had saved my life, twice. Certainly the dog was at ease with him. I took his hand. He helped me up and draped the sweater around my shoulders. I was awkwardly aware of his closeness.

"Listen," I said as we stood there, "about before... outside, on the cliff....."

"It's going to be okay," he said simply, but he was looking at me rather intently. It was as though verbal conversation did not have to happen. He already knew my thoughts, understood them and answered them. It was a strange feeling.

"Can you make it downstairs?" he inquired.

"Yes, I think so," I answered.

We moved slowly down the hall with Casey at our heels, down the stairs and into the kitchen where I sat silently, patting Casey who had placed himself next to my chair. The dog and I had only just met, but there was an instant connection between us. I watched Nicholas prepare me a meal of scrambled eggs, toast with butter and jelly and coffee. He served me, took a seat opposite mine and allowed me to take a few bites before he spoke.

"You have questions for me," he stated.

It was obvious that he knew a great deal about me. So many questions were formulating in my mind that I hardly knew where to begin. He knew this too, for he continued on.

"I am Nicholas Robert Rothchilde, your cousin, age thirty, still a bachelor. Your father's father had… no…that is too complicated. Suffice to say that we are distant cousins," he said. "And you have been blessed, or cursed, depending on who you talk to in the family, with the gift, the 'Rothchilde Gift', although from the looks of it you are still in the early stages."

"What gift?" I asked.

"You are most definitely not going mad. The voice you heard in your head was mine," he answered. "Quite simply put, several of us have the ability to communicate with each other without being in the same room and without using our physical voices. The scientists have a complicated name and definition for it. I have always referred to it as mind talking."

I had put my fork down and was sitting there staring at him, trying to take it all in. He sat quietly for several minutes allowing me to do so. No wonder we had not needed the spoken word.

"Tell me," he continued after a while, "have you been experiencing headaches or blackouts?"

"Yes," I said. "As a matter of fact I have been having more headaches than ever. As best I can figure they started after my accident in New York. That reminds me, you were there, weren't you?"

"I was there," he answered. "It has been our experience that some major trauma to the head usually awakens the power, if you will. Headaches often accompany the early stages."

"Is there no way to keep others from reading your thoughts?" I asked. "It's one thing to communicate if you wish to, but certainly some thoughts should be, are after all, private."

"Yes indeed, one should be entitled to one's privacy," he said smiling. "And yes, there is a way to keep others out. It takes practice to master but eventually it will become second nature to you."

"How do I learn more about this thing, this gift?" I asked. "I don't suppose one goes to school for instruction?"

"You will learn from me and from other family members, and there is a doctor not far from here that I used to visit with your father. He also possessed the ability to talk with his mind," he said.

"You knew my father?" I asked.

"I knew your father," he answered quietly, "and your mother."

I couldn't explain it, but I had felt a closeness to him and the fact that he had known my parents made me want to be even closer to him. I felt overwhelmed with emotion and got up from the table. I went out the kitchen door and down the path with Casey at my heels. Nicholas didn't follow immediately and I could hear him clearing the table and filling the sink to wash the dishes. I followed the stone path to the light tower. I sat down on the tower's steps looking out over the moonlit ocean, stroking the dog's soft fur.

Since the time Mr. Manning and Mr. Bell had informed me of my true identity I had been engaged in a constant struggle to keep a lid on my emotions, and I had done a fair job of holding them at bay. At the moment I was losing the battle as tears of frustration were welling up inside me that I could scarcely contain.

I had finally come home and there was some peace within me because of living in my family's house. But it was not going to be easy learning about their lives posthumously. I already felt angry at having been cheated out of the opportunity of knowing them while they were living. I selfishly felt sorry for myself because I had been denied a relationship with them and would have to hear about their lives from others who had been lucky enough to have known them. I feared the future. What was I to do with myself? Live alone in the house by the sea looking at old photographs and trying to imagine what it could have been like? How would I, who had failed at so many things, look after my father's mill? I let the tears come.

Eventually I heard Nicholas' footsteps on the path and he quietly took a seat next to me. I made no attempt to cover up my emotional outburst and he made no attempt to interrupt me, but merely put an arm around me. The dog had sensed my anguish and had settled himself between the two of us.

"I'm sorry," I managed, trying to bring my sobbing under control.

"There is nothing to be sorry for," he said quietly and calmly. "At last we've found you. Nothing else matters."

I looked at him then and he returned my gaze. There was something very comforting about looking into his eyes. I remembered feeling that way in New York. And he certainly was very pleasing to look at – he was extremely handsome.

"Ah, New York," he said. "Let's go indoors. I'll make a fire and we can have a cup of hot cocoa. This is going to take some time."

"How did you know...never mind," I finished. "The least you can do is give me a quick lesson on how not to betray my own thoughts," I said, embarrassed and wondering how much of my thoughts he had been able to read.

He smiled and laughed and in spite of myself I laughed too. The three of us made our way back up the path to the house. It was mid-September and the evening air was cool. Nicholas and the dog went through to the living room to light the fireplace and I remained in the kitchen to make the hot cocoa. I was both eager and afraid, realizing that I was about to learn the answers to some of my life long questions. When the cocoa was ready I placed the cups on a tray, and a bowl of water for Casey, and went to join them by the fire. We sat on the carpet in front of the fireplace sipping our drinks. Casey lay next to me.

After a time I set my cup down and said, "I have no idea who I am. I don't know what I'm supposed to do. I've been wishing for this moment for all my life, when I could finally belong somewhere. But I...I..."

"I know," he said calmly. "I have been keeping pretty close tabs on you and I could tell it was time to step in. I knew you would be present for the reading of the will and for reasons I won't explain now, I felt it best if I kept a discreet eye on you. It's a good thing I did – we could have lost you in New York."

"Did you see who pushed me into the street?" I asked.

He hesitated before answering. "No, I didn't," he said.

I had no reason to doubt his answer, but something about his hesitation before answering made me wonder.

"You are going to take one day at a time," he continued, changing the subject, "and I will be right here to help you through. We will bring you up to speed on the family history and you will meet some of your relatives. Everyone still living on your mother's side is within reasonable travel distance from here, so you will begin to build relationships."

"As far as the mill is concerned," he went on, "you are certainly capable of learning the business, and you will fall in love with the people who work it. It is run by fathers and their sons, families who are hard working and God fearing." He paused a moment. "Yes, my dear, your moment has finally arrived and you will do wonderfully. It's a pity we didn't find you sooner."

"We?" I asked.

"Your mother and I," he answered.

"Tell me about her," I begged.

He paused, taking a sip of cocoa. "I met her for the first time, oh, it must be nine, maybe ten, years ago. I was accompanying Uncle Nick on a trip to the mill. My own father, his distant cousin, died when I was seventeen. Besides me, my mother had three girls very close together. My father and I were very close as we had to stick together, being outnumbered by the women! When he died I took it hard and being the only boy in the family, I think my mother feared that without the proper influence I might wander down the wrong path in life. She appealed to Uncle Nick for help and he took me on, happily, I think."

"By then almost everyone in the family knew that the relationship between Uncle Nick and Max was strained. Sometimes that just happens between a parent and child. No matter what Uncle Nick did, Max didn't respond. And Max, it seemed, could do no right in his father's eyes. On the other hand, your father and I took an immediate liking to each other and he treated me like the son he wished he'd had. Back then I was too young to realize how others could be affected by our relationship, especially Max, and what new set of problems our closeness could cause," he paused, reflecting. "But because of your father, I finished high school, graduated from college and joined the family companies. We shared so many things, just like a father and son. It was the Nick and Nick show!"

I could tell by the look on his face and the sound of his voice that he truly had loved the man.

"Well," he continued, "about nine years ago Uncle Nick introduced me to the milling operation. He wanted to ease himself out completely and have me take it over. This was a real sore spot with Max, who had also finished college and was given a low level position in one of the companies. Your father and I used to travel here and spend days and weeks at a time, and it was during one of those trips that he introduced me to your mother."

"At first he called her a friend and later he confided in me, telling me of his true love for her. She was a gracious and lovely person, not only beautiful physically but the warmth and beauty of her soul...." He stopped, seeming to struggle for the right words.

"Do you know what I mean? Have you ever met someone so pleasant to be around that you can't wait for the next visit? I'm not explaining it very well, but she was an exceptional woman. It was no wonder Uncle Nick loved her." He stopped long enough to take a drink. "As time went by, she and I became friends and eventually Uncle Nick sent me here many times on my own. And then I ran the milling operation for years, until he needed me elsewhere. By then he thought Max was capable of taking it over. Max has been at the helm these last several years."

"When I was in town, I would often have lunch or dinner with your mother. As we became closer she confided in me about you and about her search for you and while I worked at the mill, I stayed here with her. With Uncle Nick's approval, I would do research for her and follow up potential leads. They wanted me to find you and get to know you. It was almost as if they knew that we were destined to…" he paused, checking himself. "Well, your mother's detective did finally find you but then your mother died before she could make contact with you and your father took up where she had left off."

My own emotions were again about to spill over. Every word he spoke was so intense I found myself struggling to hold back the tears.

"Your father was determined to bring you into the family," he continued. "He knew about your mother's wish for the attorneys to contact you on your birthday and he planned to be there to tell you his story. Your father and I have helped to take care of this place since your mother died, along with an elderly neighbor, to keep it ready for you."

"Mr. Manning said that both my parents had died in automobile accidents. But the way he said it makes me wonder if there isn't more to it," I said.

Nicholas didn't answer right away. He put another log on the fire. After apparently coming to some decision he said, "Look, it's late. There is a great deal more to say, but right now I think you'd better get some sleep."

"But Nick I …," I started in protest.

He put up a hand saying, "Now, no arguments. You've had a long day and you've learned quite a bit. There will be plenty of time for all your questions, and I promise, I will tell you everything." Seeing the look of resigned agreement cross my face, he continued, "I was hoping that tomorrow you'd allow me to introduce you to your Uncle Silas, your mother's only living brother. He has a daughter around your age and two sons, slightly older. They live about twenty miles inland and own a dairy farm. They are anxious to see you."

"They know?" I asked.

"Yes, they know," he said.

"Yes… I would like that," I said. "Nick, there is something else I would also like to do tomorrow."

"Yes," he answered knowingly. "I will take you to see your mother's grave."

"Thank you," I said, smiling. "What is it about Casey?" I asked, looking into the animal's dark brown eyes, "There is something…"

"He belonged to your mother," he answered. "She had always wanted a dog. Your father gave him to her on her last birthday before she died and he was just a puppy. I knew how much she loved him and I volunteered to care for him until we found you. You two belong together now."

"But, he's been with you for years," I protested, "I can't just tear you two apart."

At this Casey rose and placed a paw on my arm.

"Does it look to you like he wants to be anywhere else?" Nicholas asked. "Look, he and I are the best of pals and I'm sure we will continue to see a lot of each other."

I stared down at the dog. He had such a quiet and gentle demeanor. He sat there patiently returning my gaze. Here was a living being that had been loved by my mother and I somehow felt closer to her just looking into my new friend's eyes. "Casey…." I said, bending my head close to his. We touched noses and I put my arms around him.

"Well…." Nicholas started.

"Please don't leave," I begged. "I mean, you don't have to go, do you?"

"No," he said.

It was an awkward moment. I suddenly wondered what he thought about my asking him to stay. And I started wondering just why it was that I wanted him to stay. While I was trying to work all this out in my mind, he made a proposal.

"Why don't we camp out right here in front of the fire?" he suggested smiling. "Just like two cousins on an old fashioned camping trip. I'm a light sleeper, so I'll keep the fire going. What do you say?"

Frankly I couldn't have said it better. He had saved my honor and had saved me the embarrassment of trying to explain my innocent invitation to stay. I had never connected with anyone the way I had with him and I did not want to see him go.

I smiled gratefully and said, "Yes, what a marvelous idea. I'll go and get blankets and pillows." With that I picked up our cups and made a hasty retreat into the kitchen where I sighed in relief. As Casey and I climbed the stairs to fetch the supplies, I realized that Nicholas was indeed a very special man. I did not want to do anything to jeopardize our growing friendship. I had no idea what the future held for us but somehow I instinctively knew he would be an extremely important part of my life.

I gathered up pillows and extra blankets and made my way back downstairs to the living room. He had his back to me, tending the fire. He turned on hearing me enter and stretched out his hands, taking the blankets and pillows from me. He moved the coffee table and made each of us a makeshift bed on the floor in front of the fire. Quietly we proceeded to climb under our blankets, fully dressed except for our shoes. Casey cuddled in between us. For a moment we lay there facing each other.

"Goodnight Nicholas," I said. "And, thank you, so much, for everything."

"Goodnight Holly," he answered. "You are most welcome."

With that I rolled over placing my back to him.

CHAPTER

Six

Fairly early that Saturday morning found Nicholas, Casey and me headed for the town of Coopers Mills and my Uncle Silas' dairy farm. Nicholas had offered to drive us in his car, as I was doubtful that mine would make the trip. He had very politely suggested that we would have to put a trip to the local car dealer at the top of our priority list. For a moment I wondered how I could afford a new car and then I remembered the money…Nicholas had been explaining that Silas had three children Abigail, Nathaniel and Aaron.

"Max can't be too happy about the fact that I'm suddenly going to take over the company he's been running," I blurted out interrupting his narrative on the dairy farm. "Is that what you were trying to warn me about?" I asked.

He hesitated slightly before answering. "There is much to say on the subject of Max, and his mother, but I think our time now is better served familiarizing you with your Uncle and your cousins as you are about to meet them."

His answer had not been hostile and yet there was something about the way he referred to Max that convinced me there was no love lost between the two men. I realized that Nicholas possessed a great deal of knowledge about my life, and I also realized that I was becoming impatient to hear it. We were fast approaching Coopers Mills and on the outskirts of town we passed a sign saying, 'Welcome to Coopers Mills, population 1,953'.

We drove down the main street. It was Saturday morning and people were bustling up and down the main drag running errands and greeting their neighbors. There were many shops – a butcher, the barber, a hardware store, a small pharmacy, a grocery market. I spotted at least three restaurants, the town hall with attached library, the post office, a florist (conveniently, I thought) located next door to the funeral home, the police station and a gas station. One thing decidedly, and probably fortunately absent, was the presence of big business. There were no chain supermarkets or big malls. It was quaint and quiet with one two-lane road running through the center of town.

Near the edge of town we turned left at a traffic signal. On one corner stood a firehouse. It was an antiquated brick structure with two garage doors standing open. I could see a fire engine inside being polished by men who were marking time before their next call. On the other corner stood a gazebo, a large one as gazebos go, and nearby, the town clock. It was tall and black with a white face. Above the face were the words, 'Coopers Mills'.

These stood on a vast piece of land and I imagined that the townspeople would gather there to listen to a band play or to the mayor speak. The town reminded me in many ways of Henderson Point, my own new home. I felt a sudden rush, a chill of anticipation as I imagined how life would be living in such a town. It was so different from the big cities in which I had previously lived. I had always felt like just another number but now I felt I might have the chance to be an individual for the first time.

Several miles had passed when I caught sight of a large house set way back from the road. Post and beam fence edged the road and, for that matter, ran as far as the eye could see. Nicholas had slowed the car and turned in at the top of the long drive in order to step out and open the gate. The sign hanging above it read, 'Welcome to Moorehead Farm'. We passed through the gate and Nicholas stopped again to get out and close it behind us.

We drove slowly toward the house, which was a large, white gabled farmhouse with a green roof. The house was surrounded by a sea of trees and one of its most striking features was the gardens in front of it. The enormous front lawn had been divided in half, with one side a vegetable garden and the other a flower garden. Three square-topped trellises covered with climbing roses stood at some carefully calculated distances from one another on the division line between the gardens. In the distance beyond the house I could just make out fields, outbuildings and animals roaming in gated pastures.

As Nicholas stopped the car I caught sight of my uncle, his children and a dog standing on the front porch waiting to receive us. My heart was in my throat as we exited the car with Casey at our heels to follow the path to the porch.

We stopped a few feet short of the front porch. No one made a sound, not even the dogs. We stood there staring at one another. Slowly my uncle descended the porch steps and came and took me into his arms.

"Welcome, Holly," he said as he embraced me.

He was in his late sixties Nicholas had told me but it was not apparent. He had white hair and a white beard but physically he was in good shape, no doubt the result of years of working the farm. He had let me go and stepped back slightly, studying my face. He reached up his hand and gently stroked my hair. Our eyes met and I could sense the depth of his emotion. It brought tears to my eyes and left me speechless. I looked up and saw his sons and daughter smiling at us but obviously also moved by the powerful moment. Abigail was dabbing her eyes with a handkerchief and the boys were nonchalantly wiping their noses.

"Thank you for bringing her Nicholas," my uncle said, breaking the silence.

"You're welcome Silas," Nicholas answered.

"Come," my uncle continued, "please come inside."

I was so overcome I still hadn't spoken a word. He took my hand and led me up the porch stairs, with Nicholas and Casey following close behind. On the porch Abigail took my other hand. We smiled at each other, each of us trying to choke back our tears.

Inside the house was simple and clean. Coffee and biscuits and jam had been arranged on a table by the sofa. Everyone was seated and Abigail began to pour the coffee and serve the biscuits. There was an awkward moment where we sat quietly, studying each other.

The dogs had been sitting quietly but now started to move closer to each other in an effort to get acquainted.

"This is Miss Molly the beagle," Abigail said, "She is the best hunting dog in the county!"

At this Miss Molly came right over to me and jumped up placing both of her paws on my knees, as if greeting me and asking me for attention. Everyone laughed and I reached down to stroke her fur. Casey sat quietly watching the scene unfold. The beagle's innocent gesture seemed to break the tension.

"The gardens out front are spectacular," I said finally finding my voice.

"Gardening was my dear wife Ruth's passion, God rest her soul," my Uncle said. "She died not long after we lost your mother."

"I'm so sorry," I said. "That must have been a very difficult time for all of you."

"We very nearly lost Father to the heartache of it all," said Abigail. "I keep the gardens now. Mother showed me all of her secrets," she said proudly.

"Well I could certainly do with some tips," I said. "I understand that the grounds at the lighthouse were once quite lovely. I'd really like to bring back the look, but I'm afraid I'm not really good with plants."

"Oh, I'd love to help you!" Abigail offered.

"Thank you Abigail," I said, "I would really like that."

"Please, call me Abby," she invited.

The men had been listening quietly to our exchange, eating their biscuits and drinking their coffee.

"You're not going to be the only one who gets to spend time with her," Nathaniel blurted out. "Aaron and I could be useful to you girls and we'll gladly donate our muscle power to your project."

"Yeah," Aaron joined in, "we'd be glad to help. Now let's show Holly the farm."

I looked at my Uncle who nodded his head. "Yes, run along and enjoy yourselves."

I glanced at Nicholas who was smiling in agreement. "Take your time," he said.

My cousins' rose and I rose too, following them out the front door. Miss Molly and Casey rose as if seeking permission to join us so we brought them along. We spent the next hour touring the farm and as I listened to my cousins and talked with them, I realized that this must be what it was like to have brothers and sisters. They were close to my own age and unmarried. They were mature and responsible and yet they definitely possessed a child-like playfulness. They joked with and teased one another but they also complimented each other's talents and gifts. The boys bragged about Abby's cooking, baking and quilting skills. And Abby said that Aaron raised the best cattle for beef and had the best milk for cheese in the county, while Nathaniel was a master craftsman and builder.

I found myself envious of their enthusiasm for life and each other, which I would find out, did not contain itself to the farm alone. Abby said that the farm employed dozens of locals three seasons of the year thereby playing a crucial role in fueling the town's economy. She said the family felt very strongly about giving back to the community.

My tour of the farm had included seeing acres of crop fields, an apple orchard, chicken coops, the land where Aaron's cattle grazed, the barns where the milk cows were milked, Nathaniel's workshop and three ponds, which I was told were excellent for swimming and fishing. The ponds were connected by streams which were sourced by the Wallkill River. It was no wonder my cousins were still single. Their time was completely spent working the farm and interacting with the community.

"Holly, maybe you could help me on the committee for the town picnic this year," said Abby. "It's held every October and there's contests for baking and crafting and there's music and games. I am making a quilt to be entered in the contest and then used as first prize in the raffle. The committee has already begun preparing, but we could surely use you."

"Hold on there, sis," laughed Aaron, "come on up for air!"

"Yeah," agreed Nathaniel, also laughing. "Don't scare the girl off!"

"Don't pay any attention to them, Abby," I said smiling. "I would love to help you."

"Huh!" she said making a face at her brothers. She smiled at me and took my arm and we led the way back toward the house, the dogs at our heels. I found myself feeling very excited at the prospect of spending time with my new found family. They were delightful.

We rejoined my uncle and Nicholas. Before taking our leave it was decided that Nicholas and I would join the family the next day for Sunday church services, after which Abby would come over to the lighthouse to survey the grounds and formulate some ideas for what could be done with the landscape. Abby walked with us to the car.

"I'm so glad Nick brought you to us," she exclaimed. We embraced and I was again so choked up all I could do was manage a smile. She stood waving after us and I waved back until we could no longer see one another.

We drove in silence for a few miles and finally Nicholas said, "Your mother is buried at St. Justin's not far from here. Look, you've had an emotionally charged morning, are you sure you're up to visiting now?"

I paused for some time. "I would really like to see her resting place," I answered.

"Okay," he said.

We made the short journey in silence. As we drew near the church I could see the cemetery behind it. Nicholas parked the car and came around to open my door. I got out with Casey right at my heels. The air was filled with such very intense emotion and the dog could obviously sense it. I was glad to have him by my side and equally glad to have Nicholas with us. He took the lead while the dog and I followed at a discreet distance.

We walked along the side of the white, clapboard building to the rear and through the white picket gates of the cemetery. Nicholas knew exactly where he was going and all at once I saw him stop. I realized he was signaling that we had reached the place. At once my pace slowed. I had been so anxious for this moment and it was such a sad one. I had found my mother but she was not there to greet me, to hold me, to answer all of my questions, to love me.

I suddenly felt quite ill and wondered if I had the strength to see it through. I stopped in my tracks, feeling numb, like my world was once again coming to an end. I was brought back to the situation at hand by Casey. He was sitting beside me and nudging my hand with his nose. I looked at him and then at Nicholas, who had been standing there quietly, waiting for me to draw close in my own time. Somehow my feet carried me to the graveside. Nicholas stayed next to me for a moment and then silently withdrew.

I stood looking down at the headstone. 'Samantha Moorehead, Beloved Daughter, Sister and Friend, Rest in Peace'. No mention that she was a mother or a lover, but then I supposed there couldn't be. I thought it absurdly funny that a person's whole life was reduced to a few words carved on their headstone, words that really didn't even begin to scratch the surface of what and who they had been in life. There was so much more to the woman, but I supposed that all that she was in life would be kept alive in the minds of those who had known and loved her. Sadly, I was not to be one of them.

The headstone was beautifully carved with cherubs and roses. There were two urns on either side of the marker filled with fresh flowers. A freshly made wreath of multi-colored chrysanthemums lay on top of the grave.

The site was certainly kept up and I wondered who was making the frequent visits. Nicholas? My uncle and his family? I noted that my grandparents' plot was quite near my mother's and just as meticulously taken care of. I'm not sure what I expected would happen, but all at once I was overcome with the frustration of years of being alone and searching for answers. I sank to my knees sobbing. Nicholas came to my side, knelt down beside me and drew me into his arms. I remained there, crying for what seemed an eternity.

Finally I attempted to compose myself. "I'm s-sorry," I cried. "I didn't know I was going to do this…"

"No apology is necessary," he answered, helping me to my feet. "She was your mother, of course you are overcome. Let me take you home now. St. Justin's is the church your uncle attends. Perhaps you will want to visit again tomorrow with the family after services."

We were standing close together. He was supporting me with one hand and was wiping tears from my face with the other. Suddenly I realized the touch of his hand on my skin was electric. Involuntarily I took a step back and then attempted to cover up my action, and confusion, by retrieving my handbag from the ground.

"Yes," I said. "I would like that."

If he noticed my reaction he said nothing. He and Casey led the way back to the car. We made the majority of the return trip in silence. I was making a conscious effort to keep my thoughts on the visit with my uncle instead of on my evolving feelings for the man sitting next to me, afraid he would read my mind.

We were nearing Henderson Point when he said, "It's nearly half past one. Shall we stop and grab a bite?"

"Could we stop at Cunningham's store? I'd like to get some groceries and I'll make you a late lunch," I offered.

"Sounds great," he said. We proceeded to the store and while Horace and Nicholas sat in rockers on the front porch talking, with Casey at their feet, I purchased the items I wanted. After fierce insistence from Mrs. Cunningham, I accepted a freshly homemade apple crumb pie. We piled back into the car for the ride to the lighthouse.

Once there, we disembarked carrying our packages. As we neared the house, I noticed that something was sitting on the stone step just in front of the door. I mentioned this to Nick who insisted we approach more cautiously. As we got closer, I could see the object was a piece of wood. I suggested that maybe an animal dragged it there, but I could tell by my cousin's expression that he didn't think so. He picked up the piece of wood, which was a hollowed out log, and after studying it, looked from it to the surrounding forest.

Nicholas took the piece of wood and excused himself saying he would chop more wood for the fireplace. Casey and I set about preparing a lunch of chicken salad sandwiches, fresh melon and ice-cold glasses of milk. While I prepared the food, I thought about the mystery of the piece of wood left at the door. Surely no person would have done that, for what could that mean?

When the meal was ready I went outdoors to summon Nicholas. At first I didn't see him and after checking the front and side lawn finally noticed him standing by the light tower, between the tower itself and the edge of the cliff.

"Here you are," I said, "lunch is ready."

"What say we have a picnic, right here?" he asked. There was plenty of lawn between the tower and the cliff's edge so I readily agreed. It had turned into a lovely late afternoon, still warm for the time of year although one could feel the bite of cooler air riding on the breeze.

"Come," he said, "I'll help you."

We retraced our steps to the house. While he gathered up the food in the kitchen, I fetched a blanket. We made our way back to the chosen spot and set up our picnic. We sat eating our sandwiches, enjoying the sound of the waves breaking below us. A lone seagull had spotted us and was methodically circling above us, waiting for the opportunity to dive on any stray morsel.

The wind carried with it not only a touch of crisp air, but also the smell of pine from the veritable forest that surrounded the house. It was a picture perfect afternoon. Casey, having finished his bowl of food, lay on the blanket preparing for a nap. I stole a furtive glance at my cousin, noting how relaxed he looked sitting there.

"So, what is your current job with the company?" I asked, breaking the silence.

"Presently I am vice president of the mill and mining planning division, which oversees railway shipping contracts, plans for the sourcing and excavation of new mines and mills, and work as liaison between the company and the municipalities where we do business. I'm also a member of the board and a member of our internal audit committee," he finished smiling.

"My goodness!" I exclaimed. "You are certainly a busy man."

"Yes," he said, "and I love every minute of it. Speaking of work, I am going to have to check in at headquarters in New York on Monday. I will need to leave after services tomorrow."

"Of course," I said, trying to hide my disappointment. I knew he would have to be getting back to his life, but I was beginning to realize that I really liked having him around. "I'll get on just fine. Mr. Manning is coming to see me Monday and I was planning to make my way to the mill this week and introduce myself…"

"I was going to say," he interjected, "that I was planning to return here late Tuesday evening so I could take you to the mill on Wednesday for introductions," he finished.

"You don't have to rush back here," I said, trying to seem sufficiently independent. "Max has offered to…"

"I don't want you to…" he had gone from mild mannered to severely agitated and had obviously realized it, checking himself.

"What is it? What has Max done?" I asked. "You have tried to warn me about him so just what is it that I should know?"

He paused, not answering.

"Nicholas!" I said.

"Look, I don't want to speak out of turn," he said, "and I don't want to seem mysterious either. I have known Max a very long time. I realize that he is your half brother and naturally you will want to establish some type of relationship with him. You must…watch yourself."

There was undoubtedly something he was trying to tell me and why he just didn't come out with it was beyond me. I was focusing on his words, on his mind… all at once it came to me.

"He is under investigation, isn't he?" I blurted out. "That audit committee you belong to…"

He seemed startled and then annoyed and I could tell my guess was correct.

"I cannot comment on that," he said curtly. "I would ask that you have some patience."

"That's all you are going to say? Why are you shutting me out?" I asked angrily. "I am a member of the family and part of the company now too. I…"

"Holly, please don't be angry with me," he said, regaining his composure and trying to draw me over to his side. "I have promised you that I would tell you everything you want to know. I'm asking that you trust me to do that when the time is right."

He was certainly turning on the charm and I felt for the first time since I'd met him that he wasn't being completely honest with me, or more accurately, honest with me on my timetable. I was definitely annoyed but I attempted to act, at the very least, civil.

"Okay, fine," I said. "I'll just clear these dishes." I gathered the plates and glasses and stood up.

"Holly..." he started.

I made no attempt to acknowledge him and headed for the house. I quickly washed the dishes and since neither Nick nor Casey had joined me, I decided to go for a walk. It seemed that maybe we could use a little time and space to ourselves. I had used walking as a sort of therapeutic cleansing for as long I could remember. I scribbled a note, left it on the table and headed out the front door.

Much like my last walk, I found myself in front of Cunningham's store with not much of a memory as to how I'd gotten there. This time the store was closed, as it was late Saturday afternoon. I turned around and headed back. I hadn't come to any conclusions or even sorted anything out, but if nothing else, the brisk pace of my walk had provided excellent stress relief.

I could smell the aroma of a fire in the fireplace before the house came into sight. I walked up the path, under the trellis and entered through the front door. Nick and Casey were sitting in the living room. I was relieved to see that I had not chased him away.

"Enjoy your walk?" he inquired, as I hung my coat in the foyer.

"Yes, thank you, I did," I answered, sitting down in a chair. It was an awkward moment. I didn't want him to think I was ungrateful for all he'd done, and I didn't want to betray my feelings for him.

"What time did you say church services were?" I asked.

"Eight-thirty," he answered. "We'll have to get an early start."

"I had better start a light supper," I said getting up. "I thought soup and biscuits and Mrs. Cunningham's pie for dessert."

"Sounds great," Nick replied.

I busied myself in the kitchen while Nick remained in the living room reading by the fire. It was as if he sensed that we both needed a little space. When the meal was ready, we ate our soup and biscuits in front of the fire, each lost in our own thoughts. After a tasty slice of pie, Nick offered to clear and wash the dishes and I readied our bed rolls for the night.

"Right," I said, settling into my bed, "well, goodnight."

"Goodnight Holly," he said.

With that we each rolled over. It didn't feel right ending the day that way, but I had backed myself into a corner and was unsure how to get out of it. My cousin, to his credit, had not made it any harder on me. My hope for the morning was that I could start all over again.

CHAPTER

Seven

There was a great deal I did not know about my cousin, but of one thing I was fairly certain – he was a gentleman. When I awoke it was morning. I could see that he had already picked up his sleeping gear and I could smell the fabulous aroma of fresh brewed coffee. He must have heard me stirring for he came in to the living room with coffee cup in hand, which he placed on the table next to me. Casey was at his heels.

"Casey and I are heading out for a short walk," he said. "It's just five o'clock so you can take some time."

He had obviously already showered and shaved and dressed for church. I smiled at him as he and the dog made their exit, but I was afraid I could sense that something had changed between us. I was afraid he might pull back. I was fairly certain that my slight tantrum the previous evening had not been serious enough to warrant the change in his attitude, so I wondered what could have had happened. In the short time I had known my cousin I could see that he possessed a very serious, take-charge side. For whatever reason, he had donned this professional, arms-length attitude and put up a wall between us.

I was angry and frustrated and afraid of what this might mean. Just as it was beginning to feel like I might be getting a hold on my life it now felt like it was slipping away again, a feeling that was quite maddening. I was frustrated because, try as I might to pry into his mind, I could not. Although heaven only knew which of my thoughts he was able to gain access to.

I tried very hard to shut him out, but I was afraid of losing the one person who had come to mean so much to me. I had never really had time for boyfriends over the years what with working several jobs to make ends meet. Oh, I had occasionally gone out with a group of friends or had accepted the rare blind date. But my feelings had always remained casual toward any of the men I met and I often wondered what it would be like to really be in love.

Having had no previous experience to speak of, I was completely unsure of how to proceed, or if it was even acceptable for one to have feelings for one's own distant cousin. I loved hearing the sound of his voice. I enjoyed listening to the things he had to say. There was so much more I wanted to know about him.

I had managed to shower, dress and finish my coffee by the time Nicholas and Casey were coming up the front walk. The phone rang.

"Hello?" I answered.

""Holly, it's Max. I'm terribly sorry to call so early, but I thought you might be heading out to mass and I didn't want to miss you," my brother said.

"Yes, as a matter of fact I am just on the way out," I said, wondering if he had made a lucky guess or had gleaned the information through some other source. At that moment Nicholas and Casey came through the front door and the look on Nicholas' face told me he already knew with whom I was speaking.

"I was hoping to stop by on Tuesday," he said.

"Tuesday? That sounds fine Max," I answered. "I'll be here so stop in whenever you like."

"Yes, I'll do that," he said. "I'm really looking forward to spending some time with you."

"Yes, me too," I said. "See you Tuesday."

I hung up the receiver expecting to hear a verbal tirade from Nicholas. He remained silent however which only added to my confusion and frustration. We closed up the house and headed to the car to start for St. Justin's.

"I am planning to come back late Tuesday and take you to the mill on Wednesday," Nick said as we drove along. "I personally want to introduce you to Ian McKittrick, our foreman, and his son, Brian. Ian has been with the company since he was a teenager. His grandfather Rudy was the mill's first sawyer. Ian is grooming Brian to take over his job."

"It's a real family affair," he continued, "Ian's daughters Sheila and Sandra work in the office greeting customers and taking orders. Ian and your father were very good friends. They don't come any more loyal than Ian. He stood by your father through thick and thin, and he has done a great deal to ensure that the business moves forward, stays modern, but at the same time stays efficient and profitable. Ian and I have stayed in touch even though Max had been in charge these last several years."

While what he was saying was interesting, I could tell he was leading up to something.

"But…" I said.

"Yes," he answered, glancing sideways at me. "The 'but' would be that the McKittricks have found it very difficult to work with Max and his mother. Margaret has done a fair amount of poking around recently. Things did transition well when I left and Max took the helm but that was only because Ian and Brian have put their blood, sweat and tears into that business and they weren't going to let….. well, let's just say they were determined to keep things running smoothly no matter who was at the helm."

"So, chances are that because I'm Max's half-sister and a girl with absolutely no milling experience, I'm probably not going to be welcome with open arms?" I asked.

"Realistically, that supposition is correct," he answered.

"Why on earth did my father put me in such a position?" I asked. "I don't want to barge in and tell people who know what they're doing how to do their job. I won't even know what to say."

"That is why it is crucial that I take you and make the introductions," he explained. "There has been some unrest at the mill, largely led by Brian. He is the best at what he does but he is also a hot head. I don't know exactly what has fueled the fire but I am sure Brian is reacting to something, possibly having to do with Max and his mother, and I intend on getting to the bottom of it. I believe Ian and his son will accept you if I ask them to and I am going to propose that they take you under their wings and help you to understand every aspect of the business."

"Do you really think this will work?" I asked, desperate to find a way to avoid what I was beginning to think was going to be a very unpleasant situation. "Why would they bother to help me especially if they already dislike the family?"

"The short answer is that they still take direction from headquarters," he replied. "I believe I know them well enough to know that once the order is given, they will comply."

Nicholas certainly seemed sure of himself. His confidence was one of the qualities I liked most about him, I think because it made me feel so secure. He continued to talk in a general fashion about the business of milling lumber the rest of the way and, in seemingly no time, the little church came into view.

We parked the car and made our way toward the building, exchanging 'Good Mornings' with our fellow church-goers as we went. At the front door Nicholas bent down and whispered something into Casey's ear and the animal obediently lay down near the door. I was assured that we would find Casey waiting right there at the end of the service. Inside I glanced around and saw my uncle and my cousins already seated. Abby had obviously been keeping an eye on the door and waved when she saw me. As Nicholas and I approached the pew where they were seated I realized that it looked full.

"Plenty of room for you and the Mrs.," said the man sitting on the end.

The man started to rise, summoning his family to do the same. I was shocked and embarrassed by his innocent remark and very fortunately I had been in back of my cousin and so was spared from seeing the look on his face. Nicholas motioned for me to enter first. I smiled at the man and his family and climbed into the seat next to Abby. Nicholas sat right beside me but I didn't dare look at him. Instead, after greeting my relatives I forced myself to study the church and its occupants.

The building was most definitely filled to capacity, and like my Uncle's house, was simple. There were stained-glass windows, but there were no elaborate moldings or carvings, no marble floors or altar and other than the cross hanging above the wooden altar, it was a simple place of worship. As the service progressed I turned my attention to the people. Young, old, singles, couples, families - there was representation from every sector and just about every age group as well.

I thought about where I had been just the previous Sunday. Early morning walk through Central Park, several hours at the laundromat, braving the crowds for an early take out supper and a good book before bed. What a difference a week had made!

I could still hardly believe all that had happened. I looked at Abby and her brothers and found myself wishing that the moments like this would never end. I hoped desperately that this would be the start of one of many weekly traditions - gathering for church services together. I had been so preoccupied in my own thoughts and was now being nudged by Abby. She was extending her hand for the sign of peace.

"Peace be with you," she was saying.

Automatically I thrust my hand into hers and then into my Uncle's and Aaron's and Nathaniel's. Abruptly I realized that I would have to face Nicholas as well. For the first time since we'd arrived, I turned to him and extended my hand. He took it and held it, and then pulled me toward him. He whispered 'Peace' into my ear and then kissed my cheek. As he let me go, our eyes met. My heart began pounding; so much for the wall between us. At such close range I could see his eyes were green and they were kind and he was looking so intently at me, just like the day he had rescued me from the fall in the street.

A shudder of excitement passed through me and as I was still holding his hand, I knew he felt it too. I could feel the blush spread across my face. He let go of my hand and turned back to face the front of the church. I did the same trying to compose myself, hoping that my relatives had not noticed the exchange.

When services finally ended, we filed out of the building together. On the way, my uncle and his family exchanged pleasantries with their neighbors, introducing me to several of their friends. We picked Casey up at the front door and my uncle asked if I was up to visiting to my mother's grave. He explained that the family stopped there every Sunday. I agreed, but found myself as anxious about the visit as I had been the previous day.

As we approached my mother's resting place, Nicholas and Casey began to hang back. I realized that I was to be given private time with my Uncle and cousins. We surrounded the grave, with my Uncle and myself on one side and my cousins on the other.

"Well, Sammy honey," my Uncle began, "you can see that we've finally found your little girl. And I promise you, honey, we'll do everything we can to take care of her."

My Uncle had put his arm around me and with that Abby and the boys came and stood next to us. Abby took my hand while the boys touched my shoulders.

Although I tried, I could not hold back the tears. It seemed like I had done a lot of crying lately.

My uncle and his children drew close and held me in a sort of group hug and for the first time in my life, I believed I understood the love of family. While it was true that I had only just met these people, I could feel the depth of their love for me and to have someone love me and want me for their own was what I had been craving all my life. It made me sob harder and I clung to them, thanking God for this precious gift He had given me.

Through my tears I smiled down at my mother's grave, hoping that somewhere, somehow, she was seeing this moment. Eventually we composed ourselves and started back toward the cars, picking up Nicholas and Casey on our way.

"Holly," started my uncle, "the family and I would be pleased if you would consider joining us for Sunday services as a matter of routine."

"I can think of nothing I'd like better Uncle Silas and thank you," I said smiling at him.

"Well alright then," he said smiling. "Now, I know you girls are going to head back to the lighthouse now but in the future I'll expect you to head home with us for Sunday brunch. You know," my Uncle continued, "my calendar has a special note on it for next Sunday."

It only took me a moment to realize what he was referring to. It was my birthday and I realized that it would be the first time in my life that I'd spent it with family. It was obvious the others were waiting for him to reveal some information.

"Next Sunday is Holly's birthday and I say we have a real celebration for her at the farmhouse," my Uncle proposed.

"Oh yes," replied Abby excitedly. "We will do it up real good!"

"We sure will," added Nathaniel and Aaron.

"Nothing big is necessary, really," I said blushing. "Spending the day with my family will be the greatest gift I've ever had."

They looked at me thoughtfully and I could actually see it registering with them that I was in complete earnest.

"Church and family dinner it is then. Would you join us? And Nicholas too?" my Uncle asked.

"It will be my pleasure," I said and Nick nodded in agreement.

We were almost to the parking lot when the priest approached our group.

"Good Morning Silas and family," he called.

"Oh, good morning Father Meehan," returned my uncle. "Father, this is our Holly, come home to us at long last."

I smiled and extended my hand to the priest.

"Welcome Holly," the man said taking my hand into his and shaking it gently, "I am so happy that your Uncle's prayer has finally been answered. Welcome to St. Justin's and please know that my door is always open."

"Thank you Father Meehan," I said. "I will remember."

We chatted only a few moments with the man and then said our goodbyes to him and to my Uncle and the boys. Nicholas, the dog and I piled into his car while Abby was to follow us in hers.

"Well," said Nicholas as we got under way, "I am very happy to see that you are getting along so well with Silas and your cousins, not that I had any doubts that things would turn out any other way but splendidly."

"Yes," I replied. "They seem like really lovely people. I am very lucky."

"I have written down the name of a doctor whose office isn't far from the mill," he continued. "I will make sure to give it to you when we get back to the house. It's Dr. Michael Thomas, he specializes in mind talking. Your father and I have had many sessions with him through the years."

"Oh, that reminds me," I said suddenly, "if my father possessed the gift and I do, I was wondering if Max does as well?" I asked the question knowing full well that the subject of Max was likely to strike a nerve.

He hesitated before answering, but finally said, "Do you know, I am not sure. Perhaps you should ask him."

I was slightly taken back by his answer and unsure of how to respond to it, so I remained silent. I settled back in my seat and forced myself to focus on the beauty of the day. It was cold but the sun was shining and the colors of the leaves on the trees were magnificent. Two or three times during the trip I turned around in my seat to make sure Abby was behind us and she was. In what seemed like no time we had reached the lighthouse.

"Oh," said Abby as she got out of her car, "I can remember visiting Aunt Samantha here so many times through the years. It's as magical as I remember."

"Yes," I replied. "There is something enchanting about this place, isn't there?"

"There certainly is," Nicholas agreed, "and on that note I'll say goodbye to you ladies."

I hadn't thought he would leave so abruptly. There were things I wanted to say to him but not with Abby present. If Abby didn't read minds she certainly had a keen sense of intuition. She looked from one of us to the other and then announced that she was going to examine what was left of the garden she remembered helping her Aunt plant near the light tower.

"You come along when you're ready Holly. Goodbye Nick," she said hugging him, "we'll see you next weekend."

"I'm looking forward to it," he said, returning the embrace.

She headed toward the rear of the house and we were left standing there, looking at each other.

"This is not goodbye," Nicholas said.

"No, of course not," I said. "Look, I just want to thank you for all…"

"This is not goodbye," he repeated, looking at me intently.

I could feel my heart pounding like before when he looked at me, but this time rather than wait for him to pull me into his arms, I rushed into them and put my arms around him.

"Thank you for everything," I said, holding him close.

He stood there holding me and took some time before answering.

"You're welcome," he said finally. "Please call me if you need anything before I see you Tuesday. I mean it. If you need to talk or if something comes up. Here is my number and Dr. Thomas' too," he said, breaking our embrace to pull a piece of paper from his pocket. "And of course, you needn't use the telephone."

"You really think I'll be able to summon you by using my mind?" I asked.

"Well you'll never know until you try," he laughed. "You should try."

"Okay," I promised him. "I'll try."

He knelt down and gave Casey a hug and a pat on the head and then walked to his car and with the wave of his hand, drove away. I stood there staring after him. Abby's voice brought me back to reality.

"He really is a super guy," she said, coming to stand next to me.

Her voice startled me. "Oh, yes, yes he is terrific," I said, trying to act nonchalant.

We looked at each other and burst out laughing. She didn't make another comment or ask any questions, but rather locked arms with me and lead us along the path toward the back of the house, telling me of all her ideas for how to make my garden spectacular.

CHAPTER

Eight

It was early afternoon by the time Abby and I had finished surveying the landscape and making plans for the gardens. Her ideas were magnificent - everything from wild roses climbing trellises, to a man-made pond, topped off by a swing built for two to be hung from one of the giant maples near the house, and I could hardly wait to implement her ideas. I was amazed and envious of my cousin's ability to look at space and envision what it could become. Since the weather was turning colder, Abby suggested hanging the swing and building the trellises now and in the spring we would plant flowers and create the pond.

Since it seemed that we would be working on some of the landscaping and town picnic projects for several weeks, I suggested that she stay overnight with me whenever her schedule allowed and I invited her to bring Miss Molly with her. This would enable us to work longer and also get to spend some quality time together getting to know one another. She seemed to like the idea very much and also pointed out that it would allow us time to work on the quilt she had volunteered to make for the Coopers Mills town picnic.

She had very shyly mentioned that there was great demand for her handmade quilts and that the one she would make would not only be entered in a local contest but also be used as the first prize gift for this year's festival raffle. I, she said, would be her assistant thereby learning a new skill and fulfilling my duty as a volunteer. This I couldn't wait to see, not the volunteering part, but me as an assistant quilt maker – a feat I could hardly imagine myself pulling off.

Abby said her quilts had won blue ribbons for first place and various red and yellow ribbons for second and third place through the years. She was especially nervous about this year's competition as it would be judged by Laurie Levesque, a nationally famous quilter who lived near Coopers Mills and agreed to do the judging.

Abby left saying she needed to get home to do her chores and prepare the Sunday meal. She asked me to go with her but I begged off saying that I really needed to finish settling in as I had a big week ahead. She said she'd take 'no' for an answer only this once. We decided to get our projects underway that Friday and as it was going to be a very busy week for me, the thoughts of spending time with her at the end of it made me happy.

While Casey and I sat enjoying a very late lunch, I suddenly realized that I would need a place for Abby to stay. I decided that I would freshen up our grandparent's room for her and after eating, Casey and I went to look over what would need to be done.

The bed would definitely need new sheets and a new cover and I would have to pack away the personal items that remained in the room. Casey and I made a quick trip to Cunningham's to purchase bedding items and collect boxes for packing – thank heavens the store was open seven days a week! We made our purchases and were the Cunningham's last customers of the day.

Back at the lighthouse I made speedy work of gathering up the remainder of my grandparents' belongings from their room and then wondered where I'd put them. On one of the trips upstairs, I had noticed an attic door that could be pulled down from the ceiling in the hallway. I pulled on the small chain hanging down from the ceiling and at once the door came down, revealing a set of retractable stairs.

I had retrieved a flashlight from my room and used it to light the way as I cautiously climbed the stairs to find a large attic, filled with boxes. I wondered if this was where all the personal items from the rooms had been stored. One day soon I would have to go through the boxes as I suspected they would reveal a great deal about my family. I placed the boxes I had packed with the rest, pushed the stairs back into place and closed the door.

I cleaned Abby's room and made the bed with the items I had purchased. I had chosen a red and white quilt featuring a floral design with matching pillowcases. Underneath the quilt, a thick white down comforter covered crisp white sheets. I particularly liked the way the red and white quilt looked against the mahogany headboard and matching furniture in the room - it was stunning and the finished product looked quite suitable I thought.

I placed fresh towels in the rocking chair next to the fireplace. In the basket that had previously held knitting supplies, I placed logs for the fireplace. I stood at the door doing a final survey of the room's appearance. The makeover had certainly made it look fresh and clean and as I crossed the hall and looked at the room I was occupying, I knew it could also benefit from a makeover but I realized that I was not ready to remove anything that had belonged to my mother, not even the worn bedspread.

Casey and I went downstairs and I made a cup of tea, determined to turn my attention to the den. I wanted to browse through the bookshelves there. I made a fire in the fireplace in the den and was just beginning to glance at the books when the telephone rang.

I hurried through to the kitchen. "Hello?" I answered.

"Holly?" a voice asked. "This is Dr. Thomas. Nicholas may have mentioned my name…"

"Oh yes, Dr. Thomas," I said.

"I'm so sorry to disturb you on Sunday," he continued, "but I wanted to make contact with you and let you know that I would be happy to meet with you anytime you like. Perhaps this week?"

"So much is happening this week Dr. Thomas," I started. "But I am anxious to see you. Might you have an appointment available…say…on Friday morning?" I asked.

"Yes, I can be available at nine o'clock," he answered.

"That would be fine," I said. "I'll need directions."

After he gave them to me I thanked him for calling and hung up. Talking with him had made me think of Nicholas. It had been hours since I'd seen him and I had been able to keep busy. Now, as evening was coming, I wondered how I'd get through it without missing him terribly. I had better find a way, I told myself, because this was how it was going to be – him there, wherever that was, and me here alone. I looked down at Casey who was sitting at my side and I realized how grateful I was to have his companionship.

The dog and I made our way back into the den and I started looking at the books on the shelves. There were countless volumes about the weather – how to predict it, how to navigate through it, how to record it. There were some novels, mostly of the mystery variety. There were several reference books, one for gardening, one for reading and charting the stars, more than one for cooking, what appeared to be a complete set of the encyclopedia Britannica and numerous journals pertaining to the light tower.

I took one of the journals from the shelf and browsed through it. From what I could see, the keepers had kept detailed notes of times the light was tended to, household expenditures such as how much oil was used in one month to light lamps and how much ice was used to keep the icebox cold. Many of the journals were extremely old, dating back over eighty years.

I removed several more of the journals from the shelves and placed them on a table next to an over-sized armchair. I sat down in the chair and Casey curled up on the rug in front of the fireplace.

I skimmed through the volumes and came to the years where my mother had made entries. I recognized her handwriting from having looked through her address book. Her entries were as detailed as the previous keepers, although the content of the entries differed from the earlier ones. She had no need to record how much ice the icebox used or how much oil the lamps used as the lighthouse on her watch was powered by electricity. Her entries concentrated on weather at the point, temperatures and rainfall and the like, and guests that had visited. Among her callers had been cousins, school friends, acquaintances including Father Meehan, Nicholas and even a former teacher. If my father had been a regular, his name had been omitted.

I put the books down and sat quietly focusing on the fire. I thought about the nights that Nicholas and I had camped out in front of the fire and I wondered where he was. I closed my eyes and tried to clear my mind, thinking of nothing but him. Suddenly the answer came.

Am home safely, will call tomorrow.

I started and opened my eyes fairly certain that we had just communicated, like the times I had heard him in my head before. Maybe this mind talking wouldn't be as difficult as I'd imagined.

I sat there staring blankly at the bookshelves in front of me and all at once my eyes caught sight of a large, black book. I rose from my chair and headed straight for it. Even before my hand touched it I knew that it was the family bible. I carefully removed it from the shelf and carried it back to my seat.

I gingerly turned the yellowed pages until I came to the family history section of the book. There before me lay my genealogy or as much of it as my relatives knew of or had bothered to record. I saw Peter Joseph Moorehead's name listed as the family's founding patriarch. No wonder his magnificent portrait still hung over the mantel. Notably absent from the pages was my name and I felt saddened and then angered by the omission.

As I sat there thinking about it I realized that of course there could be no mention of me – I was illegitimate and given up, not the sort of thing one would probably record in the family bible. That made me wonder if my mother might have kept a personal journal. She was obviously an excellent record keeper and I made a mental note to ask my Uncle Silas and Nicholas if they recalled any such personal journals.

I had been sitting for quite some time and as night had fallen, decided to get a quick breath of fresh air before preparing for bed. Casey and I went out the front door and sat on the step. I tried to clear my mind and looked out over the moonlit water and at the dark blue sky with its stars that sparkled like diamonds. Instead of sitting down by my feet Casey remained standing, cocking his head this way and that. He was definitely acting as if he was bothered by something.

"What is it boy?" I asked. "What's wrong?"

He turned his head and looked at me and then turned back looking in the direction of the trees. His repetition of this movement began to make me feel uneasy, as if he were trying to warn me of some impending danger. I looked intently in the direction the dog was watching but try as I might, I could only see the soft swaying of the trees in the light breeze. I suddenly remembered the piece of wood that was left on the doorstep. I quickly stood up and we went inside, locking the door behind us.

"It'll be okay boy," I said, trying to reassure him as much as myself. "We'll just check the locks on the windows and on the kitchen door and then we'll have a sandwich and get ready for our busy week."

The dog's demeanor had seemed to shift from alert mode to the calm and easy manner he usually displayed. I wondered, however, just what could have been out there to upset him - another animal, or perhaps a person? I ruled out the latter telling myself that no one would have any good reason to lurk around the lighthouse.

Casey and I had a light supper, tidied up and retired early. I found sleep impossible as my mind not only played over the events of the last several days, but also fantasized about the days to come. What would Mr. Manning have to tell me? What would it be like spending time with Max? What kind of reception would I receive at the mill and would I ever fit in there? And what of Nicholas? No matter how much thought I gave any of the questions plaguing my mind, the answers were not to come.

CHAPTER

Nine

That Monday morning I awoke feeling rather happy despite all of my unanswered questions. At least my life had taken a direction and I was eager to follow the paths presenting themselves to me. I showered, dressed and watched the national and the local news, trying to bring myself up to speed on what was happening in the world and learn something about what was going on in my community. I saw an advertisement on the local channel for the upcoming town festival in Coopers Mills and smiled looking forward to the time I would be spending with Abby making our quilt. Casey and I had breakfast and I was heading toward the front door to take him for a walk when the phone rang. I opened the door and let him into the yard before running back to the kitchen to answer the phone.

"Hello?" I said.

"Good morning Holly," It was Nicholas.

I said, "I got your message last night."

"I'm glad," he said. "Next time you must try to say something back."

"Yes," I agreed, "I will try, I promise. I spoke with Dr. Thomas last night and I am going to see him on Friday."

"That's very good. I know you will like him," he said, "and he will really help you fine tune your skills. I could make arrangements to go with you if you'd like."

I had been listening to Nicholas and I suddenly heard the screen door opening.

"Oh," I said, "I think Mr. Manning may have arrived for our appointment," I added, stretching my neck to bring the front entry into view and stopping mid-sentence as I realized that my caller was not the attorney, but rather Margaret Rothchilde. She had not bothered to ring the bell but had walked right in and now was standing there as large as life in my living room. There was nothing friendly in her demeanor at all and in fact, I felt that everything about her reeked of evil.

Somewhere in my subconscious warning bells must have started pealing. I could hear Nicholas' voice desperately calling to me through the receiver.

"Holly....Holly, are you there? What's wrong? I know there's something wrong, please answer me," he was shouting.

"Margaret...." I said finding my voice as I stood there staring at her. "Margaret Rothchilde is standing in my living room," I said trying to remain calm.

"Alright," he said pausing a moment, "alright, tell her that I'm on the phone and that I'd like to speak with her. When she takes the receiver, leave the house. Do you have your car keys?"

"I...yes...they're in my pocket," I answered, thrusting my hand into my coat pocket to feel the keys.

"Okay, now do as I've said," he instructed urgently.

The woman had not taken her eyes from me and was slowly, steadily moving toward the kitchen where I was standing. I lowered the receiver and offered it to her as I called, "Mrs. Rothchilde, my cousin Nicholas is on the line. He would like to speak with you."

She stood there staring at me for some time before speaking.

"I have come for you," she said taking another step toward me.

"No, please," I cried, retreating up against the kitchen door. I was still holding the receiver and could hear Nicholas shouting into it. I felt a wave of nausea sweep over me and in the distance I could hear Casey barking.

I heard the screen door open and close again. Mr. Manning walked in followed by Casey who quickly placed himself between the woman and me. It took Mr. Manning only a moment to size up the situation.

"Margaret," he said calmly, "I didn't know you'd be visiting this morning."

"Gerard," she said acknowledging him, turning her attention from me. "I was just leaving," she said and with that she quickly departed.

Mr. Manning watched her exit and then was by my side in an instant. I handed him the receiver as he helped me into a chair.

"This is Gerard Manning," he said speaking into the device. "Nicholas…...no, she has gone. I'll see to Holly, but something will have to be done. Yes….yes, that's a possibility, but let us talk about that at length later, I'll call you…….yes, of course I will…...she's right here, I'll ask her."

To me he said, "Nick would like to speak with you."

I was badly shaken but put the receiver to my ear.

"Nicholas…." I said.

"My God, are you alright?" he demanded, and continued without waiting for my answer. "Look, I'll be there this afternoon. Don't worry, everything is going to be okay."

"Can you spare the time?" I asked, "I'm sorry…"

"When will you understand how much you mean?" he started. "I will make arrangements and I will be there in a few hours. Gerard will stay with you until I get there."

"Thank you," I said.

"See you soon," he said and rang off. I stood up and placed the receiver back in its cradle. Mr. Manning took me into his arms and held me.

"There now," he said, patting my hair, "it's going to be okay. Nicholas and I will talk with Margaret. She can be difficult, but I am sure we can get her to come around. Please don't be too upset. Here now, let me fix you a cup of tea and then we'll have a long talk."

He led me through to the living room and deposited me onto the sofa. He shut the front door and returned to the kitchen. I heard him rummaging through cabinets and filling the teapot with water. Casey sat on the couch snuggled right next to me and shortly the attorney returned carrying a tray with the teapot and two cups.

"Look, we can postpone the financial business until a later date," he said pouring the tea, "You have had a most trying morning."

I thought about what he said and then answered, "No, I think I'd rather focus on the business you came to discuss. We should go ahead and take care of the financial arrangements and I know there is something you want to tell me. I'll be alright, it's just that I was startled at seeing her and she seemed so…so…strange," I finished.

"Yes," he agreed handing me my cup, "she can be a force to be reckoned with but it was entirely inappropriate for her to call on you in that way. Nick and I will take care of this my dear."

"You know my cousin?" I asked.

"Yes, for some time," he said pausing to sip his tea, "I had the pleasure of making his acquaintance, oh, years ago. Your father introduced us and as you probably know, Nick played a key role in searching for you."

"Yes, he did mention that he had been involved," I said.

"He was a great source of comfort to your father," he said. "He was a son and a confidant and a friend."

"How long do you suppose Mrs. Rothchilde knew about the affair, and about me?" I blurted out.

"Well," he said, "my dealings throughout the years were mostly with your father as he was my client. I really only knew Margaret in a social sense, nothing more than that. It's possible she could have suspected there was another woman for quite some time, women often sense these things. As far as you are concerned, I believe she only learned about you shortly before your father's death. He told Margaret and Max at the same time."

"Oh that must have gone over really well," I said dryly.

"Actually, it was rather a scene," he said returning his cup to the tray. "Your father had asked me to be present because he wanted to tell Margaret and Max about you and he wanted me to discuss how bringing you into the family would impact them on a financial level.

Margaret was terribly upset. Max took it more calmly, and as I reflected on it later, it almost seemed to me as though he wasn't the least bit surprised. Although, I don't see how he could have known anything about you. Your father kept his most private papers locked away in my office. Well, in any case, it would be wise of you to be on your guard against the both of them until we know exactly where they stand."

"That reminds me," I said putting my cup down, "that first day in your office you made a comment about the way my mother and father died as being a 'strange coincidence'. What did you mean by that? Are you suspicious of something, is that what you want to tell me?"

He regarded me intently and then said, "It's nothing I can put my finger on. It's just that something doesn't feel right and little bits of information don't add up. I keep hoping that the puzzle pieces will fit together and I will have the answer," he finished.

I must have looked thoroughly confused so he said, "Please don't worry. Just keep your eyes open around Margaret and Max. This has been a difficult time for them and when things settle down I'm sure we'll get the answers."

I knew he was trying his best to reassure me, but I made a mental note to try to find out as much as I could about the Rothchildes and to try to force the puzzle pieces together.

"Now," the attorney said, "why don't I drive us into town? The bank there is the one that your mother used to handle all of her financial transactions and Mr. Bell has taken the liberty of phoning ahead so they will be ready to receive you and set up your accounts. Also,

Mr. Bell wanted me to inform you that your mother had some money left in her accounts there that will be transferred to you. He has given me all of the necessary paperwork to submit to the manager. We didn't have time to tell you about this the day your father's will was read."

With that Mr. Manning rose and deposited the tray in the kitchen, escorted Casey and me to his car and drove us to town. The bank manager received us graciously and guided us through the reams of paperwork necessary to transfer my mother's accounts to me and to set up my checking and savings accounts. Although he presented a knowledgeable and tenured air, I caught him wide-eyed and gasping at the zeros behind the numbers in my new accounts, something I was doing quite a bit of myself.

A couple of hours later when our work was accomplished, Mr. Manning declared he was going to take me to lunch. After leaving Casey at the front door of a small luncheonette on the main street called Cathy's, we entered and found a seat.

The kindly attorney declared he would order soup and sandwiches for us at the counter. I chose a booth near the front window and sat waiting for him. The café was beginning to get busy. I looked around, studying my lunch companions. All at once, the sound of a conversation taking place in the booth behind mine caught my attention.

"What do you think Ian will do about it?" asked one male voice.

"I don't know," answered another male voice. "Why should anyone care about a bunch of hollow logs anyway?"

"It's not that they're worth a lot," said the first voice. "It's just the idea that someone would steal them."

"Now we don't know that," replied the second voice, "animals could very well have dragged them away or maybe the girls sold them and forgot to write it down. Look we'd better finish here, make that delivery and get back to the mill."

I was fascinated by the conversation and sure that the men must have been talking about my mill. I thought about the hollow log left at my doorstep and wondered if that could have been left as some message to me. At that moment, Mr. Manning came toward the table carrying a tray with our food on it. I rose to help him set our table. As we seated ourselves and prepared to enjoy our lunch, the men from the booth behind me rose and headed to the counter to pay their bills. I had only a few moments to study them and would have to mention what I'd heard to Nick to see what he could make of it.

After we'd eaten, a waitress retrieved our dishes and served us coffee.

"Mr. Manning," I said as I stirred my coffee, "I want you to know how grateful I am to you for taking such good care of me and my interests. I really feel that you are taking the best possible care of me, and I wanted you to know how secure that makes me feel."

He looked at me and I could tell he was moved by my words. He paused before speaking.

"Holly, my dear," he said, "I am pleased that you are feeling good about the way your affairs are being handled. This has to have been very difficult for you, learning about your mother and father and brother, and now trying to carve a life out of what you've learned. If in some small way I am able to help you through it, it is my privilege."

"I would like you, and Mr. Bell of course, to be my attorneys, officially," I continued. "I hope that will be okay even though there is quite a physical distance between us."

"I know I speak for Mr. Bell when I say that we would be honored," he said. "And don't worry about the distance. It is easily handled by the quick commuter flight and the rental car," he said smiling.

"You know," he continued, "things will start falling into place. I have a feeling that now that you are here, things will happen. Tell me, what have you got planned for the rest of the week?" he asked, laying money down on the check. We rose to depart. We stepped out into the brisk sunny air. Casey immediately got up and joined us.

"Well, Nicholas is introducing me at the mill on Wednesday and I have an appointment with Dr. Thom…" I cut myself off, realizing that I would have to explain.

"Is that Dr. Thomas?" he asked, opening the car door for me after depositing Casey in the back seat.

"You know then?" I said as he shut the door.

He seated himself in the driver's seat before saying, "If you are referring to your family trait, the mind talking I think Nicholas calls it, yes, he and I have spoken on the subject," he answered, buckling himself in and starting the car.

"Have you ever heard of such a thing?" I said.

"My dear," he said as he skillfully navigated the car along the winding road, "hardly anything would surprise me. You can always find some peculiar or unique trait in almost any family. And certainly telepathy is a well documented one in the annals of history."

"Tell me, do you know if Max possesses the gift?" I asked.

He paused before answering, and I saw a look come over his face like it did when he had stated that my parents' car accidents were a strange coincidence.

"Honestly, I'm not sure," he replied. "Have you been able to actively use your power?"

We had driven out onto the point and before I could answer, we noted that a car was parked there. Upon seeing us, the driver exited the vehicle. It was Nicholas. Mr. Manning brought our car to a stop and in a minute I was out the door and into Nicholas' arms. Mr. Manning got out and opened the rear door so that the dog could greet Nick too.

"How did you get here so fast?" I asked.

"Company helicopter," he answered holding me, "and a fast rental car waiting for me at the air field."

He let me go and extended his hand to Mr. Manning.

"Gerard," he said, shaking the man's hand, "thank you for taking care of her."

"Anytime, Nicholas," the man said, smiling. "Well, young lady," the attorney said to me, "as you are in good hands, I will be getting back to New York. I will check on you in a few days and I will let you know how I make out with Margaret. And Nicholas, I'll phone you later."

"Goodbye," I said hugging him on impulse. "And thank you for everything."

When he had gone, Nicholas and I started toward the house. Almost simultaneously, we noticed the front door standing open.

"You didn't leave it like that, did you?" he asked.

I shook my head.

"You stay here. Casey and I will check this out," he said.

"Nicholas…."

"Stay here," he commanded. He opened the screen door and he and the dog disappeared inside the house.

I passed a few anxious moments continuously looking over my shoulder. I moved closer to the house and noted that the front door appeared to be just opened, not forced or damaged in any way. Just then Nick and the dog appeared.

"Everything seems to be in order," he reported, opening the screen door for me.

"But that makes no sense," I commented, entering the house. "Why break in and take nothing? And speaking of that, looking at the front door makes me think someone used a key. The lock doesn't looked forced."

"I don't believe this was an ordinary break-in," he said.

"But what, then? Why?" I asked. I remembered how Casey had acted uneasy the night before and mentioned this to my cousin.

"It may be just an attempt to rattle you, to upset you," Nicholas answered.

"Who would do that? Who else could have a key?" I asked.

"I can think of one or two people," he replied. "But let's not worry about that now. I'd like to stay here a few days with you. We will have the locks changed. Maybe we can set my computer up in the den."

We surveyed the room, deciding it would make a satisfactory make-shift office. While I cleared away items from the desk top, Nicholas made several trips to and from the rental car to retrieve papers, a small computer and monitor. Casey had placed himself on the rug near the fireplace and was keeping a watchful eye on us. When I'd finished with the desk, I went through to the kitchen to make tea. Upon my return, my cousin was seated at the desk, arranging his papers. I placed the tray on the table near the fireplace and sat in one of the chairs facing it.

"You look all settled in," I observed, pouring the tea.

"Yes, thank you," he replied. "I am sorry to take over your space like this, but think my presence here is necessary just now." He paused and then asked, "Did Margaret say anything to you?"

"No, not really," I answered searching my memory. "She was suddenly in the room and the dog was barking and Mr. Manning came in soon after that. She just stared at me in the strangest way."

"How do you mean?" my cousin asked, getting up from the desk and coming to sit in a chair near me.

"It's hard to describe," I said, handing him a cup of tea. "She seemed almost like she was in a trance. Wait, I think she did say something. It was… 'I want you'… no, it was, 'I came for you'. There was a very strange atmosphere in the room. I know that isn't describing it very well but that's the best I can remember."

Nicholas sat thoughtful, sipping his tea. "Let me think about this and a course of action. Why don't we have a light supper, turn in early and tomorrow we can spend time preparing you for your trip to the mill on Wednesday," he suggested.

I agreed readily to his plan despite all of the questions plaguing my mind. I believed I knew my cousin well enough to know that he would know what to do and would share it with me when the time was right. For tonight I would prepare dinner and spend a pleasant evening with him. Later as we prepared our sleeping bags in front of the fire, I said a silent prayer asking for the courage and strength to face the days ahead.

CHAPTER

Ten

We rose early, had a light breakfast and walked the dog. Nicholas retired to the den, turned on his computer and declared he would work there for a couple of hours. I busied myself with some light housekeeping and then made a couple of telephone calls. I called Cunningham's store and placed a grocery order to be delivered later that day and during the course of the conversation found out that Horace was also the local locksmith. He agreed to change the locks to my front and back door that afternoon when he delivered the groceries. Next I called Abby to confirm she could come over Friday afternoon and stay overnight. After checking with her father, she agreed happily and said she would bring some materials that we could use to start work on the quilt we would be making.

It was late morning and I was in the kitchen making coffee for Nicholas and myself when I heard a car entering the yard. I went through the living room and peeked out the window to see my brother Max behind the wheel. All at once I remembered it was Tuesday and he was scheduled to visit.

I went into the den and told Nicholas, who was not happy about the news but said that Max must not see him there. Nicholas didn't offer any reason as to why Max shouldn't see him but said he would stay quietly upstairs until Max left. I didn't question my cousin's motives and he slipped out of sight. I tidied the desk in the den and pulled the pocket doors closed just as there was a knock at the front door.

I forced myself to relax and smile as I opened the front door.

"Hello Holly," Max said.

"Please come in Max," I replied opening the door wider.

He entered and we took seats in the living room.

"I know I said I'd call first, but I had to be in the area on business today and thought I would take a chance and just stop by. This is really a beautiful place," Max observed. "How are you getting on here?"

"Very well, really," I answered. "I am getting acclimated to the house and the neighborhood, and I can't believe I get to enjoy this incredible view every day."

"Have you bought a car?" he asked, motioning toward Nicholas' rental car that was parked in the yard.

"Oh no," I said, trying to think fast. "It's just a rental as mine isn't working very well."

He regarded me intently then, as if sizing me up and I noticed that his eyes kept looking toward the ceiling, almost as if he suspected we were not alone. The silence was awkward and almost becoming unbearable when he spoke.

"Listen, Holly" he started, "I want to apologize for the way my mother barged in here yesterday." I was about to protest but he kept on. "Oh yes, I know about it. Mr. Manning called to tell me and when I asked mother about it, she didn't deny it. She hasn't been right for quite some time. She goes off for hours at a time without telling me. There have been a lot of strange incidents lately and she has been making some odd statements."

I was listening very carefully and began to actually feel sorry for him.

"Does she live around here then?" I asked.

"We do have a home a few towns away in New Windsor," Max answered. "It's sort of a vacation cabin. We aren't there year round – our permanent home is in New York. I stayed at the cabin while I was running the mill. I built it so I would have a place to stay while I was stationed here working."

"Please let me know if my mother does or says anything to upset you," he continued. "I was hoping that we could forge some type of decent relationship. It will be harder for her to do that, but I don't see any reason why we can't work on it."

"Yes, I'd like that Max," I answered, trying to placate him.

"Have you been to the mill yet?" he asked.

"Not yet, I'm going later this week," I said, trying to stay vague.

"Well, I'd love to come and work with you there anytime or help out in any way I can," he offered. "I really enjoyed my time there."

He certainly sounded very genuine and he seemed pleasant, but I wasn't quite sure what to make of him. He must have sensed that he hadn't won me over and decided to keep the interview short. He rose, glancing at his watch.

"Well, I must be off as I have an appointment not far from here," he announced.

I rose too, moving toward the door.

"Thank you very much for coming to see me," I said, opening the door.

"I hope to see you again soon Holly," he said as he paused in the doorway. For a moment I thought he might try to embrace me. If he was thinking about it, he decided against it and moved out into the yard toward his car.

I stood in the doorway waving after him until he drove off the point.

When I turned back into the room, Nicholas was standing there.

"It's hard to know what to think about him," I remarked. "He seemed sincere but I almost feel like he was on a fishing expedition. What could he hope to learn from me? I know nothing. Once or twice I had the feeling he knew someone was upstairs, although you didn't make a sound. And the talk about how much he enjoyed his time at the mill…I thought you said that he and the employees didn't get on that well."

"I can see you are a good judge of character," Nicholas commented. "He and his mother bear watching. Actually, it might be a good idea to ride by that house in New Windsor just to make sure no one is staying there, although I assume Margaret must have come from there when she came here Monday." With that my cousin opened the doors to the den, walked to the desk and sat down at his computer. He offered no further insights on the Rothchildes.

As it was early afternoon, I went to the kitchen to prepare lunch. I made sandwiches with a side of macaroni salad. I set the little table outside the kitchen door and then called to Nicholas when everything was ready. We sat enjoying our modest lunch when for the second time that day, I heard a car drive onto the point. I stood up and made my way through the house to the front window where I could see Horace Cunningham stepping out of his truck.

"Hello Horace," I called out to him as I opened the front door.

"Good day," he replied pleasantly.

I made my way toward the truck preparing to help carry the bags when Nicholas walked past me, greeting Horace.

"Good afternoon Horace," he said smiling. "Please let me help you with these bags."

"Never turned down an offer of help," Horace said with a smile and handed two bags of groceries to my cousin.

"We were just finishing lunch Horace, can you join us?" I asked him as he himself brought two bags of groceries through to the kitchen.

"I thank ye kindly for that offer, miss" he said sincerely, "but if I don't change your locks and get the rest of these groceries around to the folks waiting, Mrs. Cunningham's going to have some words for me!" he finished with a smile and a wink.

Nicholas walked with him back to his truck. My cousin helped carry tools to and from the doors for Horace as he changed out the locks. I went to the kitchen to stow away the groceries. In no time at all, Horace was handing me new keys.

"Remember, if you need any more keys made, just let me know," Horace said as he headed toward his truck.

"I will Horace and thank you so much for taking care of this so quickly," I said.

He smiled and drove off waving his hand out the window.

"What a really nice gentleman," I commented as we made our way back to the kitchen.

"He truly is," remarked my cousin. "Horace reminds me a bit of Ian McKittrick. Are you excited about tomorrow?"

"Excited and anxious and nervous," I replied. "What more can you tell me about the mill?"

"I believe I've told you enough for now," answered my cousin. "I think you should meet them and form your own impressions, size up the situation and then we can compare notes."

I turned to look at my cousin and saw he was in earnest. I would have to wait until tomorrow. With the groceries stowed away, we turned our attention to clearing the lunch table. Nicholas announced he would retreat to the den to get a few more hours of work in. I knew I was storing up a great deal of anxiety over my trip to the mill and declared I would take a walk. My cousin was about to protest, but I said I would bring the dog with me and that we wouldn't go too far or too long as the sun would be starting to sink soon, and he reluctantly agreed.

I headed out into the afternoon air bundled up. Although the sun was shining, it was an unseasonably cool afternoon. Instead of heading toward town as I had done on previous walks, I decided to follow a path I had seen that ran along the cliff overlooking the water. As I got nearer the cliff, I could see a steep footpath carved into the cliff. The footpath was bordered on one side by forest and on the other by the sheer drop overlooking the water. The footpath was plenty wide enough, although I had to watch my footing because of the occasional rocks and roots.

Casey and I strolled leisurely along for some time when suddenly we could hear movement in the forest. Casey began barking at once and clearly wanted to head into the trees. I called him off and insisted he follow me home. He obeyed but kept a watchful eye on the tree line. All at once I could actually see movement in the trees.

I began running up the path back toward the lighthouse with Casey at my heels. In my mind I tried to communicate with Nicholas to inform him of our predicament. As we got closer to the lighthouse, we met him on the path – I had been able to communicate to him. Nick surveyed the tree line but we saw no one and there was no sound. We walked in silence the rest of the way home.

Back at the lighthouse, try as we may, we couldn't really come up with an explanation for what had happened. We put it down to an animal, maybe a bear or a moose although I don't think either of us really believed that. We kept our thoughts to ourselves, had an early dinner and stretched out on our make-shift beds by nine o'clock.

CHAPTER
Eleven

On Wednesday morning, I rose early, even before Nicholas. Casey and I crept quietly into the kitchen to begin coffee-making preparations. While the coffee was brewing, the dog and I slipped out the kitchen door and made our way toward the light tower. I stopped about halfway down the path and turned toward the ocean to watch the sky. The sun's light was just starting to illuminate the horizon. I wrapped my housecoat around me as a chilly breeze swept past me. I could hear the sound of the waves breaking far below me. The air was invigorating. Casey sat next to me taking it all in.

As I stared at the beautiful scene before me, I wondered what the day at the mill would be like. I had tossed and turned all night worrying about what had happened on the cliff path and what my reception would be like at the mill. Whatever it was, I was resolved to meet it with a calm determination. I wanted to make my mother and father proud of me, wherever they were. I wanted to prove myself to my Uncle Silas and my cousins. And thankfully, Nick would be by my side.

I turned to make my way back to the house and called to Casey to follow. As we reached the kitchen door, I saw that Nicholas was in the kitchen pouring coffee into cups. As he prepared our drinks, I filled Casey's water bowl and put food in his dish.

"Sleep well?" my cousin inquired.

"Yes, okay," I lied, determined to maintain a calm air, although I didn't fool him for one moment.

He gave me a raised eyebrow and a smile. "Don't worry," he said. "It really will be okay."

"How long a trip is it to the mill?" I asked.

"We should leave here after breakfast," he replied. "It will take us about twenty-five minutes."

We enjoyed homemade cranberry muffins with our coffee. They had been made by Horace's wife and sent along with my last grocery order. When we had finished eating and washing up, I retreated upstairs to wash and dress. I had decided that simple elegance would go a long way today. I pulled on a sweater, skirt and boots. I checked my reflection in the standing mirror. Satisfied with my look, I took a deep breath, gathered up my coat and purse and headed downstairs to join my cousin. He was sitting at the kitchen table and smiled as I came down the stairs.

"Ready?" he asked.

"Yes, ready," I answered.

He called to Casey who immediately got up from his cushion and followed us through the front door. After making sure the door was locked, we made our way to the car. We drove away from the house and at the end of the driveway, made a left turn. We stayed close to the coastline the entire trip. The landscape along the stretches of the narrow two-lane road had ocean views on one side and forest and fields on the other.

After only fifteen minutes of driving, I could see that we were entering a town. A large wooden sign on the side of the road read, 'Welcome to Berne, Home of the McKittrick Family Sawmill'. I questioned Nick about the mill's name, wondering why it didn't bear the Rothchilde name. He explained that even though it was a Rothchilde subsidiary, my father had felt strongly about leaving the original name intact out of loyalty to the McKittrick family and all that they had come to mean to him. I felt the excitement well up in me as I knew it would not be long before I would see the legacy my father had left to me.

Nicholas skillfully navigated the car through the winding, hilly seaside town. Down and down we went as we made our way closer to the water's edge. Finally he turned the car off the main road. After traveling through dense trees and down a long dirt driveway, we came out on a sort of large peninsula of land surrounded by the ocean on two sides and on the third side by a fast running stream with a thunderous waterfall which ran out from the forest and emptied into the ocean. Nicholas explained that the stream was fed by the Furman River, which narrowed to become the stream and waterfall before emptying into the ocean.

The mill was a good size and sat near the waterfall side of the peninsula. The two-story structure itself was made of wood and painted green with a silver-colored metal roof. A huge water wheel was attached to the side of the building that stood next to the Furman waterfall and it was spinning around continuously. I surmised instantly that the wheel must power the mill and I could see that a metal chute attached to the building also received water from the wheel.

Logs were coming out of an opening in the mill and traveling down the chute and into the ocean with the help of the water. Men were wading in the water below and corralling the logs. A rock jetty, almost forming a circle, created a kind of shallow pond in the ocean where the logs were kept. There was an opening in the jetty wall and that was where the pond and ocean met. A sign above the doorway read, 'McKittrick Mill, Est. 1905'. There were several other smaller buildings on the property which Nicholas explained housed tools, machinery and trucks.

Nicholas parked the car near some others and we got out with Casey at our heels. Casey seemed familiar with the place as he took off to greet some men who were stacking lumber. Nicholas explained that they were inserting slats between the piled lumber because it's never flat piled. It needs air flow in between to prevent mold. As we approached, the men stopped their work to greet us. Just then, the door to the mill opened and several people came out. A couple of curious on-lookers came to the door to watch the scene unfold, but did not come out into the yard.

"Hello Ian!" my cousin called as he walked up to a man and shook his hand. "Ian, may I present Holly Snow, Mr. Rothchilde's daughter. Holly, this is Ian McKittrick, whose family has helped operate this mill since its' founding."

I smiled at Ian as I studied him. He had greying hair and a weather-worn face that was deeply tan. He was maybe late fifties or sixty, but very fit. Ian stepped forward. He removed his hat and wiped his hand on his overalls.

"Welcome Miss," he said extending his hand to me. "We are pleased to know you."

I took his hand into both of my hands as I said, "Mr. McKittrick, it is indeed an honor to meet you."

He looked slightly taken back and our eyes met as he studied me intently for a moment before a large, warm smile began to spread across his face. He took me gently by the arm and began to present me to the others.

"Miss, this is my son Brian and my daughters Sandy and Sheila. They work along-side me here at the mill." Brian took a step forward and shook my hand without saying a word. The girls both smiled, shook my hand and wished me welcome.

"Well now, let's head inside and we'll give you a proper tour," Ian said motioning for us to enter the mill.

The group made its way inside with Nicholas and Casey following. Inside, there was a wooden platform about eight feet wide that nestled against the walls and ran around the whole interior. Stairs down from the platform in several spots led to where many pieces of equipment used to manipulate the lumber sat on a concrete floor. The fabulous aroma of fresh cut wood penetrated my nostrils.

Activity in the mill had ceased at our arrival and now men were scurrying back to take up their positions and start work once again. Ian asked Brian to go and tell the men to take a twenty minute break so the noise made by the machines wouldn't drown out our conversation. Brian went at once to carry out his father's order.

There were also stairs upward which I was told led to another platform from which one could observe mill operations and from which one could gain access to offices and the break room. From the upstairs, you could also access the waterwheel that helped to power the mill and the chute assembly. Ian explained that logs on the floor that were to be moved by sea were fed onto a conveyor belt that led up to the chute which carried them away to the ocean corral assisted by the water. Downstairs there was a business office that could be accessed from the outside and where customers could place their orders. Sandy and Sheila worked in the office greeting customers, taking orders and then communicating the orders to Ian and Brian.

Ian explained that his grandfather Rudolph had picked the location because of the power that the waterfall could provide to the mill and the proximity to the open water. Wood could be transported by land and by sea, the latter being used to move extremely large volumes of logs to another location where they could be loaded onto trucks and hauled away. Ian said that the trucks needed to haul extremely large loads could not be brought through the small town or onto the peninsula. Large orders were corralled in the pond and then moved down the coastline by tugboats to a place where the logs could be moved onshore again and loaded on trucks for delivery.

Ian sent Sandy and Sheila back to work in the office and then led the way up a set of stairs and let me take in the sight below. I peeked over the rail and observed the equipment and conveyor belts from above. It was an interesting vantage point. I caught sight of Brian talking to several men and pointing up at us. I had a feeling that although Ian had genuinely seemed welcoming, Brian might have very different feelings about me. Ian had opened a door and was ushering Nicholas and Casey into a small meeting room. I quickly joined them.

"Best to let the men take a small break now," Ian explained. "The saw is quite loud when it's running. Why don't we sit down and talk?" he continued.

We had just taken our seats when the door burst open and Brian came in. He shut the door hard behind him, which startled the dog and me. The air in the room was filled with tension.

"Have you asked her what she plans to do with us?" Brian demanded of his father.

"Sit down boy!" Ian commanded in a firm voice. "Have you no manners?"

Brian looked angrily from his father to me, but said nothing as he took a seat.

"Please excuse him Miss," Ian said apologetically. "He is young and too hot headed for his own good sometimes."

I looked at Nicholas. He met my glance. I heard the words *Go Ahead* in my mind. I smiled at him for giving me the chance to handle the situation and to start developing a relationship with these people.

"I understand how he feels," I said slowly and calmly. "For a stranger to come here and suddenly take over, and for a girl who knows absolutely nothing about the running of a mill at that." Although I spoke kindly, my words were blunt. It was the issue at hand and now it was out in the open. I had Ian's and Brian's attention – they were both looking at me very intently, waiting for what would come next.

"I have no intention of changing anything here," I continued. "I only ask that you would allow me to observe and to learn. I would like to understand this business and how it works and maybe someday, I could make some small contribution."

Ian said, "That is fair. You can spend time with the girls learning the front office and you can watch and learn what happens on the floor. Besides knowing the milling part of the business, Brian takes care of our books and he can go over them with you. He went to the local college and got a degree in business," Ian finished proudly. Although Brian looked none too happy about what his father was suggesting, he said nothing.

I agreed with Ian's proposal and then stood up and thanked Ian and Brian for their hospitality. Ian said that I should start my mill education with the girls in the front office. We walked downstairs to the office where he put the plan to the girls who were very excited and agreeable and worked out a schedule whereby I would come to the mill every day for the rest of September and all of October and November. I would work with the girls in the office until lunchtime, after which I would have a chance to observe work on the mill floor and have some time to go over the books with Brian. After November we would evaluate my progress Ian explained, and we would see how much work was coming in for the winter months.

We said our goodbyes and as we were leaving, equipment on the floor was started back up and I was surprised at just how noisy it was. Nicholas said that I would be given a pair of ear plugs to help protect the ear drums and keep the noise to a minimum – they were standard issue for all mill employees. We headed toward the door, thanking Sandy and Sheila as we went.

As we stepped outside, we passed two men talking and overheard one asking the other the whereabouts of some inventory. I recognized one of the men as being the same man I heard talking about the mill in the café, the day I had lunch with Mr. Manning. He was the one who had been telling his friend about the missing hollow logs. As we walked towards the car, I noticed that Casey kept looking towards the woods and cocking his head, the way he had done at the lighthouse and on the cliff path. And then I noticed Nicholas also studying the tree line.

"What is it?" I asked him, feeling uneasy.

"It's nothing," he answered. "Probably some animal."

I suspected that my cousin wasn't telling the truth but we'd reached the car and climbed in.

"How about some lunch in town?" Nicholas was saying. "I know a great little café."

"Oh yes, please!" I said. I hadn't eaten much that morning due to nerves and now was famished.

Nicholas navigated the car to a charming café that overlooked the water. We left Casey by the front door. After we had placed our order, my cousin complimented me.

"You did beautifully today," he said, making me blush. "You were kind and respectful but firm. They will love you in time."

"Do you think so?" I asked. "Ian and the girls may come to like me but I'm not so sure about Brian."

"Don't worry about Brian, he will come around," my cousin replied confidently. "Holly," he continued, "the Rothchilde cabin isn't far from here, do you feel up to driving over and checking it out after lunch?"

I hesitated only a moment. "Yes," I said thoughtfully. "I think it would be a good idea for me to know exactly where they are. What if someone is home, how will we explain our presence?"

"I will just say that I am showing you the cabin so you know you have family close by in case of an emergency," he responded.

I raised an eyebrow and we both started laughing.

"I seriously doubt that they would want to help me," I said, wiping my mouth.

We finished lunch, paid our check and picked up Casey as we made our way to the car. Nicholas informed me that the town of New Windsor was just a ten minute drive away. He negotiated the narrow, winding roads skillfully and in no time, we were turning off the main road and onto a dirt driveway. We slowly drove along until the house came into view. Nicholas stopped the car and said we would continue on foot.

As we got out of the car, I stopped to study the house. It was not what I would call a cabin. True it was made out of logs but it was more like a miniature mansion – large and grand – and it was completely surrounded by trees, so much so that daylight hardly penetrated through the canopy overhead, giving the scene a dark and foreboding atmosphere. We walked slowly toward the house with Casey at our heels. There was no car present and no sign that anyone was home.

"Nick," I whispered, "I have a very uneasy feeling being here. Can we leave now?"

"Yes," my cousin replied, "there is nothing more to do here at the moment. You know where it is now."

We retreated toward the car. I let Casey into the back seat and as I was opening my door I glanced at the house one more time. I believed I caught sight of a movement near one of the windows on the first floor. I hurried into the car but said nothing to my cousin. He backed our car slowly out of the driveway and turned it toward the lighthouse.

"So," I said, "they really don't live far from the mill or the lighthouse."

"It is true, they don't," my cousin responded. "But there is no reason for either of them to be living here on a full time basis now. Margaret prefers her house in New York and Max's current job has him stationed in New York as well."

I sat thoughtful on the remainder of the ride home, thinking about Ian and his family and the mill. How interesting it would be to go there every day and learn about the business of milling. Once back at the lighthouse, Nicholas retired to the den to spend some time on his own work. I did some light cleaning and laundry and began dinner preparations. We had an early supper and Nick went back to his work. As dusk was falling, I went out into the yard and stood watching the sun set. I told myself I would never tire of the sight of the sun setting over the water, it was truly magnificent.

As I turned around to head back into the house, a movement among the trees caught my eye. All at once I could see someone moving among the trees. Instead of heading for the house, I ran straight toward the moving figure yelling for Nick to come outside as I went. As I was nearing the tree line, Nicholas and Casey came out the front door and headed in my direction.

"What is it?" my cousin called, as he joined me.

"I saw someone moving among the trees," I replied.

"Are you certain?" he asked.

"Yes, I was sure," I said. "I don't know where they

could possibly have gone without our seeing, so maybe I am mistaken,"

Casey had been standing still but was listening intently and suddenly started moving away from us barking. We followed him through the trees, almost around in a circle until he came to a stop near a cluster of big trees near where the drive opened onto the point.

"What is it boy?" my cousin asked, patting the dog.

The dog was standing near a particular tree and then sat down next to it.

Nicholas and I looked at the dog and then at each other.

"What do you suppose he is trying to tell us?" I asked.

"I'm not sure," my cousin answered slowly. He began to study the tree, looking up among its branches and then began walking around it. Suddenly he stopped.

"What is it?" I asked, coming to stand next to him.

"Look at this," he said, reaching his hand out toward what looked like a handle attached to the tree. As he slowly pulled on the handle, a portion of the tree bark opened like a door. Shocked, we stepped forward to look inside. A portion of the huge tree trunk had been hollowed out just enough to make room for a person to stand inside.

Nicholas went in first and then backed out, motioning for me to try it. Once inside I noticed there were two small holes around eye level that once looked through, gave an excellent view of the house and any comings and goings on the point. The discovery sent chills up and down my spine. I backed out the makeshift hiding spot.

"Obviously someone is using this spot to spy on me and the house," I started. "I don't know whether to be more angry or more scared."

"This is truly disturbing," my cousin said.

"What should we do about this?" I asked, very concerned. I could see that Nicholas was extremely upset about the discovery although he was downplaying it.

"For the moment, nothing," he answered. "I think it may be best not to let anyone know that we have discovered this. Let me give some thought to the best course of action."

With that, we made our way back to the house. Nick went to the study and I went to the kitchen to start dinner. As I worked, I thought about the day – the trip to the mill and the discovery in the forest. The more I thought about that, I realized that someone could hide in the tree, but they must have used transportation of some sort to get out here. I made a mental note to search along the property for a place to conceal a car.

As we ate dinner, I realized that the excitement of the day had made me tired. My cousin had picked up on this too and insisted that I turn in early while he handled the cleaning up. I gratefully accepted his offer. I prepared our sleeping bags in the living room and then laid down on mine. Casey came and snuggled in next to me. I was asleep in seconds.

CHAPTER Twelve

On Thursday it was decided that Nicholas would drop me off at the mill, run errands, head back to the lighthouse to work and then pick me up around five o'clock. I looked forward to seeing the girls and to smelling the wonderful aroma of fresh-cut wood. At the mill, Sheila and Sandy welcomed me warmly. I settled in and observed them greeting customers and taking orders. Orders were placed for all sorts of things – logs for the fireplace, wood for building fences and houses and new custom kitchen cabinets and fireplace mantels, sawdust for gardens and chicken coops. I realized how ignorant I had been to the many uses of wood.

Sandy and Sheila explained that they used every piece and bit of lumber. I was amazed at how many products the mill produced and sold. The girls expertly handled every situation and I commented on this. They laughed, explaining how they had been working in the mill since they were teenagers. In addition to my watching and learning, the girls introduced me to each customer. Brian had come in one or twice to review the new orders and I had the feeling he was really trying to size me up and see how things were going.

I was feeling determined to win Brian over. Once when he entered the office, I tried engaging him in conversation.

"Brian, how do you know what to do out there in the woods?" I asked. "How do you know how to harvest trees?"

"Every woods tells you how to cut it," he answered. "If you are in touch with nature and respectful, the woods will still look beautiful even after you finish. You must think forward to the future as you harvest trees. It is an art that takes some time to develop," he finished. He went on to say that the mill handled lumber that was brought in to be cut but also that he and his father would bid to do a job of cutting trees or clearing lots.

I could tell by the way he spoke that he was very passionate about the work. He seemed almost embarrassed by the passion of his answer and excused himself, heading back in to oversee the running of the various machinery on the mill floor.

At lunchtime, the girls and I ate sandwiches together and then I went outside to stretch my legs. As I looked around the property, I saw employees stacking wood and preparing orders for pickup. Others were working on the wood that had been corralled in the water waiting to be moved south. The girls had explained that the men used long poles to move the logs around in the corral. When it was time to drive them south, logs would be bound together in groups and then the tug boats, with the help of log drivers, would move the logs south along the coast to an area where they were loaded onto trucks and then delivered.

All at once, I caught sight of the employee that had made the comments about the missing hollow logs. He was talking and gesturing to a coworker. I walked casually in their direction, hoping to overhear the conversation. I got just close enough to hear the coworker telling the employee not to worry about the logs, and then the employee turned away saying he needed to use the telephone. I was tempted to move forward and talk to the employee who was worried about the missing logs, but just then the office door opened suddenly and Sandy called out to me. I retreated to the office but made a mental note to discuss the situation with Nick.

Though the work day was not over for everyone, the girls let me go daily around five o'clock. I reminded them that I had an early doctor's appointment the following morning but should be in to work by ten o'clock. Nicholas arrived to pick me up and as he opened the door, Casey jumped out to greet me.

"Hello Casey," I said as I bent down to stroke the dog's fur.

"Have a good day?" my cousin inquired, smiling.

"Yes, it was a great first day," I said.

The ride back to the lighthouse passed with me giving my cousin a summary of all of the things I had learned that day. As we approached the driveway, I asked my cousin to drive past slowly and explained my idea about looking for a place to hide a car. We drove slowly looking at both sides of the road. Almost simultaneously, we both noticed a turn off the road that looked like a driveway, but it was only a dirt path that stopped in between some trees maybe some twenty feet off the road. There was no car present but fresh tire tracks were obvious. It was a very good spot to put a car and it was within walkable distance from the lighthouse driveway.

Satisfied with our discovery, we turned around and headed back to our driveway. As we drove out onto the point, I noticed a strange car parked there. I turned to question Nick and he flashed a big smile at me.

"That is your new car," he said proudly. "I went car shopping for you today!"

"What?" I exclaimed. "You didn't have to do that. You shouldn't have paid for it."

"Why not?" he responded. "It's a welcome home gift."

"Oh Nick," I said, "it's too much. It was very thoughtful of you but you must let me pay you back."

"I wouldn't think of it," my cousin replied. "I'm allowed to give you gifts," he said looking at me so intently that I found myself fidgeting in my seat. I opened the car door and got out to inspect the new vehicle more closely.

"Well," I said humbly, "I am most appreciative. It is beautiful." I had never owned a new car nor had anyone ever purchased a car for me. I was overwhelmed. The car was a brand new silver-colored Volvo, cross country wagon. It would certainly be able to handle the terrain and it had plenty of space for Casey, other passengers and storage.

"I'm thrilled that you like it," he said. "The dealer will come and collect your old car tomorrow – I wanted to give you time to remove any personal items from it."

After admiring the car, we went into the house and started dinner preparations. While dinner cooked, I cleaned out my old car and readied it for pickup. It was early evening as I carried the last of the items from the car toward the house. As I did, I caught sight of someone standing at the foot of the driveway. The figure was a good distance from me and I couldn't make out if it was a man or woman.

I shouted for Nick, dropped the items I was carrying and ran in the direction of the figure. As I approached the spot where the figure had been standing, it was empty – no sign of anyone in any direction. Nicholas and Casey came running up behind me.

"What is it?" Nick asked, slightly winded from running.

"I was sure I saw someone standing here," I said. "Let's check the hollow tree."

We made our way to the tree and looked inside but found nothing.

"Quickly," Nick said, "let's check that spot in the woods."

We ran up the driveway to the road, with Casey at our heels. We could hear the sound of a car and as we ran down the road toward the spot we had recently discovered, we caught sight of a car motoring away from us on the road, but we hadn't actually seen it come from the place in the trees.

"Listen," said my cousin as we walked back to the house, "now seems a good time for me to show you something. Let's get the rest of your things from your old car inside, lock up the house and then we can go."

We did just as he said after removing dinner from the oven and covering it until our return. We locked the door and with Casey at our heels we started walking toward the cliff.

"Where are we going?" I asked.

"You never have to feel trapped here. The foot path you started down the other night leads to the beach where I keep a small but sturdy motorboat. I want to show you the way in case you ever need to use it. We can actually motor to the mill from there, it takes about ten minutes by boat," he explained. "I keep the boat in the water till late October or first snow, whichever comes first, and then I motor down to the mill and store it there for the winter."

Casey and I followed him across the yard and almost to the edge of the cliff where we picked up the footpath. My cousin explained that someone, probably the first keepers of the lighthouse, had dug out the path so they could have access to the beach. The path was wide enough but steep and muddy and filled with small rocks and roots. One definitely had to watch one's step. We descended quickly enough though and in no time were standing on a small beach. There was a motorboat tied up at the end of a short pier.

"This is amazing!" I said. "What a great escape route. Can we take the boat to the mill?"

"You really want to?" Nicholas asked.

"Yes, I do," I said. "I'm not sure why but I feel like I should know how to do this."

"Alright then," he responded, "we should be able to make the round trip in about twenty minutes."

After helping Casey and I on board, my cousin took the wheel, started the craft and we were off. Nicholas explained that staying close to the shoreline was the best way to proceed. As we motored along, I gazed at the beautiful but wild shoreline. Eventually we rounded a slight bit of land and rocks that jutted out into the sea and the sawmill's peninsula came into view.

Nicholas explained that it was possible to maneuver the boat near the mill and park and secure it to the mill dock. The mill looked deserted and peaceful.

We turned the boat around and started the return journey. The water was fairly calm. Nick lit two small lanterns attached to the boat so that we could see and be seen. Once back at our own dock, we secured the boat and made the trip back up the cliff via the footpath.

As we reached the top, the house came into view. At once, we saw another car parked on the point and we could see two people sitting on the front steps of the house. As we drew closer, our guests stood up to greet us and we could see that it was Max and his mother.

Follow my lead, I heard in my head and I glanced at my cousin who returned my gaze with a smile.

"Well, Max, Margaret, what a lovely surprise!" Nick called.

"Hello Max. Good evening Mrs. Rothchilde," I said, following my cousin's lead.

"Well, where have you two come from?" Max asked. "I hope we're not interrupting anything," he said in an almost accusatory tone.

"Not at all," Nicholas replied. "I was just showing Holly the footpath down to the beach. It's a beautiful night for a walk. Please come in, let's have a drink."

Although Nicholas had his own key, he stepped aside holding the screen door open, waiting for me to open the wooden front door. After opening it I stood back and allowed them to pass through. Once inside the foyer, we hung up our coats and moved into the living room. The situation was immediately awkward and tense. Even Casey seemed to be on guard, sensing the tension. Nick sat down and this seemed to indicate to the dog that our visitors were okay. He sat beside Nick but didn't take his eyes off our guests.

"Please have a seat," Nick offered, "What brings you here at this hour?"

"Holly, I really just wanted to check in and see that you were doing alright and that everything is going well at the mill," Max answered as he and his mother sat on the couch, "And what are you doing here at this hour Nicholas?"

Max had asked the question innocently enough but it was obvious that he and his mother couldn't wait to hear the answer.

"Ian and Holly called me in to discuss some equipment replacement at the mill so I'm in town for a day or two. I thought I would spend some time with Holly in the evening while I was here," Nicholas responded. "This seems an odd hour for you to arrive from New York," he added.

I was beginning to feel that I was watching two fighters in a ring, circling and sizing each other up before throwing the first punches.

"Well, I just couldn't get away from work early today, so it has delayed my arrival time getting here," Max answered. "Mother is visiting some friends in town this weekend so I offered to bring her and thought I could check on Holly."

"Can I get you something to drink?" I offered.

"No thank you Holly," Max said standing up. "We really must be going," he added as he turned to help his mother up.

We moved toward the foyer where they collected their coats and we followed them outside. We had gotten just outside the door when Margaret declared she had left her handbag on the couch. I offered to dash back inside for it. I found it just where she said it was and as

I turned to go join them outside, I saw that Margaret had followed me inside. She was standing there much like she had been on Monday morning.

"Why are you still here?" she asked. "You must leave here now."

With that, she took her handbag from me and retreated out the door. I followed her and watched her get into the car with Max. Nick waved as they drove away.

"Well, what do you make of that?" he asked as we made our way back inside.

"Margaret just told me to leave," I answered, explaining what had just happened in the living room.

Nick tried to make light of the visit and told me not to worry. But I caught him in deep thought several times as we reheated the dinner that I made earlier. After dinner, he retreated to the study to work and I chose a book from shelves in the study and settled in the living room by the fire to read until bedtime.

CHAPTER
Thirteen

On Friday, Nicholas, Casey and I set off early for Dr. Thomas' office. It was actually in the Town of Berne and not far from the mill. Nicholas explained that Dr. Thomas was a general practitioner, with a specialization in neurology and psychiatry. I couldn't imagine how a man with such advanced education ended up practicing in such a small out-of-the-way town. While I was looking forward to meeting the doctor, I was also a bit nervous. I felt a little like a specimen about to be placed under the microscope.

When we reached town, we drove down the main road and then turned off onto a side street. The doctor's office was attached to his house. We parked on the street and exited the car. As we approached the house, the door opened.

"Good morning Dr. Thomas!" Nicholas called.

We continued up the steps and onto the front porch.

"Hello Nick, hello Casey," the doctor greeted us, reaching down to pat the dog. "And this must be Holly," he continued, taking my hand.

"It's very nice to meet you Dr. Thomas," I said, shaking his hand.

The doctor held the door open for us and then we followed him down a hallway and past a woman sitting at a desk who acknowledged us with a smile. The three of us were ushered into a small examination room.

Nick made himself comfortable in a chair and Casey settled next to him on the floor. The doctor indicated that I should take a seat on the examination table. He looked into my eyes with a bright light and tested my reflexes. I believe I expected him to start performing experiments on me, but all that followed was conversation.

How was my head feeling, when did the headaches start, what did I know about telepathy, had I been able to communicate with my cousin – these questions and others about my general health took up some time. The doctor was just beginning to speak on the topic of telepathy when there was a knock at the door and then the door opened slowly. The nurse peeked her head into the room.

"I'm very sorry to disturb you doctor," she said gently, but urgently. "Ian has called from the mill. He asks if you can go there immediately – there's been an accident."

At once Nicholas rose from his chair, followed by Casey and I got off the table. The doctor crossed the room to pick up his medical bag.

"We'll meet you there Dr. Thomas," my cousin said. The doctor nodded his head without saying a word.

"What could have happened?" I asked as we quickly made our way to the car.

"I don't know," Nicholas replied. "Ian has been running that mill a long time and aside from the small cut and bruise, we haven't had any bad injuries. It can be a dangerous job, but fortunately we have never had any serious injuries."

Nicholas drove as quickly as he could and I noted that the doctor's car was right behind us. As we drove down the road leading to the mill, we could see sheriffs' cars, an ambulance and people standing around.

Ian spotted us and walked straight toward the car. Nick stopped and we opened the doors. I could tell by the look on Ian's face that something was terribly wrong.

"Nicholas, it's bad, very bad," Ian began. He looked at me. "Miss Snow, the last thing in the world I want to do is upset you. Maybe you should wait here."

"Whatever has happened Ian, I am going to go through it with you," I said as calmly as I could. He looked proud and worried at the same time.

"What is it?" my cousin asked.

Ian motioned for us to follow him. We made our way through the crowd of employees, customers and police to find a man lying motionless on the ground, on top of a blanket. His body and clothes were wet. The doctor moved past us and went at once to the man's side. He knelt down and put his fingers on the man's neck. He looked up at us and shook his head.

As I looked at the man, I realized that he was one of the mill's employees – in fact the very employee that I had overheard talking about the missing lumber. As I stood numb, trying to process what was happening, a man in uniform approached us.

"Hello Nick," he said, "I'm very sorry about all of this."

"Thanks Adam," my cousin replied. "Holly, this is Sheriff Adam Dineen. Adam, my cousin Holly Snow is the new owner of the mill. She has just moved here to learn about its operation and take over managing the business."

"It's a pleasure to meet you Miss Snow," the sheriff said shaking my hand. "I'm sorry it has to be under these circumstances."

I nodded, unable to find my voice.

"What do we know Adam?" Nicholas inquired.

"Employees opened as usual. This employee, Mike Carter, was seen floating among the logs in the water corral. As soon as he was spotted, some of your men took long poles and moved logs so others were able to go in and haul him out," the sheriff reported. "He isn't wearing his waterproof overalls, so we don't think he was working in the corral when this happened."

Just then, the doctor joined us.

"He's wet and he's been moved. I will know more after the autopsy, but right now I'd say he's been dead eight to ten hours."

"Can you tell how he died doc?" the sheriff asked.

"In his current condition, it's hard to tell," the doctor answered. "I will know more later."

Nicholas quietly explained that the doctor was also the local coroner. He had practice rights at the hospital twenty miles away. The doctor asked that his station wagon be brought closer so that the body could be loaded into the back of it. The sheriff directed several of his deputies to assist the doctor.

Nicholas turned to me. "Holly, are you alright?"

I hardly knew what to say. I knew that Ian and the rest of the employees must be feeling very upset.

"Nick, I'm alright," I started. "If Sheriff Dineen will allow it, I think we should get everyone inside. We need to calm people down."

Nicholas moved away to speak with the sheriff. Ian was standing with his children. I approached them.

"Ian," I said gently, "Nicholas is asking the sheriff if we can move everyone inside. Are you all okay?"

Sheila and Sandy had been standing near their father and looked absolutely shocked. Brian was standing nearby, very quietly but obviously taking everything in.

At that moment, the sheriff asked for everyone's attention. He asked that everyone move inside, be seated and wait to be interviewed.

At this Brian spoke up saying, "We are going to lose a whole day of work."

His father looked at him angrily but did not speak. Instead we moved toward the door like everyone else. Once inside, I took Ian and the girls aside.

"Look," I said, "we might be at this for a while. Can we order some sandwiches and drinks from the local café? I will be responsible for the bill."

Sandy looked at her father and then at me. "That is very kind of you Holly. I know Kristin at the café. I could call her and explain the situation and ask her to deliver the food. Is that okay?"

"Yes Sandy," I answered. "Order whatever you think we'll need. Maybe we can set the food up in the break rooms and offices upstairs. Sheila and I will help you. I think if we can keep everyone calm and comfortable this will move along."

I excused myself to go and find Nicholas. He and the sheriff were overseeing the moving and resettling of the employees and customers. I told them that food and drink were being ordered and brought in to make everyone more comfortable.

"And there is one more thing sheriff," I said. "The

dead employee is the one I overheard talking about missing logs. Nicholas, I had been planning to tell you about this but being so new to this business myself I'm not sure if what I overheard has any significance or not. Now that he is dead, I am wondering if there could be any connection."

I proceeded to tell both men where I had been and what I had overheard. The sheriff took notes while Nicholas remained silent, but I could see his mind racing.

We will discuss this later I heard in my head and I realized that my cousin was giving me a message. It was very strange that he was standing right in front of me but he clearly did not want to discuss the matter further in front of the sheriff. Our eyes met and I signaled that I understood.

Before I knew it, it was noon. The food arrived and the girls and I served the group and tried to make everyone as comfortable as we could. The sheriff and his deputies called each person and took a statement from them. Some interviews were slightly longer than others. By two o'clock, the sheriff announced that everyone was free to go. He would follow up if needed but his next move was going to be to check in with the doctor.

As Ian and Nicholas and I stood talking about the day, Brian approached us.

"Several of the men have offered to stay and work for a few hours. We have some big orders to fill at present and I think we should take them up on their offer," he said.

Ian and Nicholas looked at me. I could hardly believe they were leaving the decision up to me.

"Brian," I said, "please thank them for their loyalty. Let the employees know that anyone who would like to stay and work is welcome to do so. Anyone too upset by today's events may leave, with pay, and return to work tomorrow."

Brian hesitated only for a second, then nodded and left to carry out the instructions.

"Holly," Ian started, "I'm so sorry your first days at the mill turned out this way. I can already see that you're a natural. You're calm under pressure and you're compassionate. I thank you for your kind handling of all of us today."

"Thank you Ian," I said smiling.

At that we heard the equipment on the floor start up. Nicholas whispered something to Ian and then motioned for me to follow him. We made our way downstairs to the store front. After making sure that Sheila and Sandy were okay, Nicholas told them that we were going to follow up with the doctor and that we would see them in the morning.

As tomorrow was Saturday, the mill would be open from eight o'clock until one o'clock in the afternoon. Outside I questioned my cousin about whether we should open on Saturday considering the circumstances. He thought about it for a moment and then said that he thought it best to remain open to help everyone stay busy and focused through the difficult time.

On the ride to the hospital to see the doctor, I asked my cousin what the significance of the hollow logs could be. Although he said he wasn't sure, I could tell that it bothered him very much.

At the hospital, the doctor came to greet us and by the look on his face, I knew we were not about to hear good news.

"Dr. Thomas," Nicholas started, "have you been able to tell what caused the accident?"

"This was no accident," the doctor replied looking very grim. "Mr. Carter died from drowning. What got him into the water in the first place was a nasty hit on the head. He was hit from behind, probably rendering him unconscious, and then tossed into the water. Based on the trajectory and nature of the head wound, I believe someone struck him. I don't believe he tripped, hit his head and fell into the water. Secondary injuries include internal and external damage from being crushed between the logs but I believe those occurred post mortem."

For several minutes, no one said a word. My brain stung as the words 'not an accident' played over and over in my mind.

"So, you're saying someone killed him on purpose?" I asked finally finding my voice.

"It looks that way," the doctor responded. "I have reported my findings to Sheriff Dineen."

"Did he have a family?" I asked.

"The sheriff said he lived in town alone," the doctor answered. "His parents live a few towns over. The sheriff was going to see about notification to the family."

Nicholas thanked the doctor and I promised to make another appointment to see him as our session had been interrupted by the morning's tragedy. I was suddenly exhausted and very glad when my cousin suggested that we head back to the lighthouse. The ride back passed in silence as each of us sat lost in thought about the day's events.

It was early evening when we reached the lighthouse. As we got out of the car and approached the front door,

I could hear the telephone ringing. I opened the door and hurried through to the kitchen to answer it.

"Hello?" I said breathlessly.

"Hello Holly, its Max," I heard a voice say into the receiver. I hardly knew what to say to him, how to tell him about the awful events of the day. I was spared from bringing up the subject.

"I've heard what happened at the mill, are you okay?" he asked.

"Max, how did you hear about this already?" I asked. At my question, my cousin threw me a concerned glance and I knew instinctively not to give out too much information.

"My mother was in town today as the news spread. Of course she called to tell me. What happened, what is being done?" he inquired.

"Right now Max all we know is that it was a terrible accident," I lied as calmly and convincingly as I could. "The sheriff is investigating and we will hear more eventually."

My answer seemed to satisfy him and Nick was nodding his head as if approving of what I was telling Max.

"Well, please keep me informed. If I can do anything for you, don't hesitate to call," he said.

"Thank you Max, I will," I said and I hung up the receiver. "The news has travelled fast," I said to my cousin. "Are you surprised that Max knows already?" I asked.

"Nothing about Max would surprise me," Nicholas answered. "Margaret is supposed to be here visiting her friends. Maybe they were in town when the news broke."

Before I could answer, we heard a car driving onto the point. I went to look out the front window and saw it was Abby arriving.

"Oh, it's Abby," I said. "I had completely forgotten she was coming tonight."

"Holly, I think it best that we say nothing more about this tonight, especially in front of Abby," Nicholas replied. "I don't want her to be concerned and you and I could certainly use a break. We'll be dealing with it again tomorrow."

I agreed with him and then flung open the door and ran out to greet Abby. She was certainly a welcome sight after the day we'd had. She stepped out of the car and Miss Molly jumped out after her. I helped her with her bags. Nicholas and Casey gave them both a big welcome. Abby and I went upstairs to put her bags in the room across from mine and then headed downstairs to spread her quilting supplies out on the dining room table. Nicholas announced that he would make us dinner and he took the dogs and retreated to the kitchen.

Abby had chosen a pattern for the quilt which she said would be titled 'Storm at Sea' and tonight we would be washing fabric, cutting material into the pieces used to make the quilt and ironing and starching the material. After the day I'd had, I was very content to listen to Abby talk about the happenings at the farm during the week and her brothers' latest escapades while we carried out our tasks.

Abby said that her brothers were busy building a swing and wooden trellises for my yard from lumber they had cut down on the farm. I felt honored that there would be pieces of their farm at the lighthouse forever, and could hardly wait to see their finished products and see them placed in my yard.

Nicholas' announcement that dinner was ready brought us into the kitchen where we found a delicious looking meal of pasta and meatballs with salad and bread. We showered him with compliments. Over dinner, Abby talked about how to cut fabric and about the many steps involved in quilt making.

She talked about the woman who would be judging the entries, Laurie Levesque. Abby spoke of her with great respect and reverence as her work was nationally known and said that all the local quilters aspired to be like her and hoped to put forth a creation that she would deem to be the best.

After dinner, Nicholas offered to clean up while we retired to the dining room to continue work on our project. While we had dined, the fabric had been put in the washer and then the dryer. The measuring and cutting of the fabric took a long time and the work was pain-staking. I was very impressed with my cousin's meticulous determination. After ironing the fabric, I passed it to Abby. She used design templates that she had created from cardboard to measure and mark the material. After cutting it, she passed the pieces back to me for starching and ironing.

When Nicholas had finished the cleaning up, he looked in on our assembly line with a smile and announced that he and the dogs were going to the den to work. After working long into the night, we all finally decided it was bedtime. Abby and I retired to the front two rooms upstairs and Nick stayed in one of the back bedrooms. Miss Molly stayed with Abby but Casey took turns sleeping first with me and then with Nick.

I was up early Saturday morning and made a large breakfast for Nicholas and Abby. After we ate, we helped Abby pack her bags and bade her goodbye, saying we'd see her tomorrow at church.

As Nicholas washed up after breakfast, I ventured out the kitchen door and followed the path to the light tower with Casey at my heels. I sat on the steps and gazed out over the ocean, listening to the waves break against the rocks below me.

I thought about Abby and the festival and how proud she was to be submitting her quilt. All at once, I had an idea. I got up and hurried back toward the house.

"Nicholas," I said, as Casey and I entered the kitchen, "I've had an idea about the festival. What about having some representation from the mill? Could we have some kind of entry?"

"What a great idea," my cousin said with a smile. "We could have a log rolling contest and a log cutting contest. We can also donate wood for the fire pits that they have placed around the festival. And several of our employees are expert carvers. They use chain saws to fashion items out of wood. They could demonstrate how that's done and bring some of their carvings to sell."

"What kinds of things do they make?" I asked.

"Believe it or not, they can carve animals, like bears, eagles and moose from wood," my cousin answered.

"Oh my goodness!" I exclaimed. "I'd like to see that. In fact, I would like to have a piece of art like that here in the house. How can we find out if the mill can participate?" I asked excitedly.

"I tell you what," Nick said, "I will telephone Abby and ask her who I should contact on the committee. While you're at the mill this morning, why don't you mention this idea to Brian and Ian and see if they like it? We can report on our progress when you return this afternoon."

We agreed to our assignments and I said goodbye to my cousin and Casey and headed to the mill. When I arrived, it was business as usual. If I hadn't lived through the drama the day before, I never would have known that anyone had just died there.

I found Brian and Ian in the office with the girls and put mine and Nicholas' ideas about the festival to them immediately. For a moment, there was silence and I was afraid they didn't like the idea.

"I think that's a fine idea," Ian said smiling.

"Yes, I agree," said Brian, nodding his head. "We've never done anything like that before, but maybe it would be good for us to participate. Come inside to the floor with me Holly. I'll introduce you to some men who could help us with this."

Brian held the door open for me and we went inside. Once on the floor, Brian motioned for the men to stop the machinery, which they did at once. He called them over to us and told them of the idea. Several men volunteered to participate and even said they would be thrilled to show off their work. As I listened to the men, I noticed Brian was watching me. He smiled at me when I looked at him.

I thanked the men for their enthusiasm and willingness to help and promised to give them more details after I had spoken with the festival committee. With that, Brian had them get back to work.

I could hardly wait to tell Nick about the response at the mill. When I got home that afternoon, I told him of Ian and Brian's overwhelmingly positive response. Nick said that he had spoken with Abby who had in turn called one of the festival organizers. The mill would be a welcome addition to the festival and the committee was excited to have such an interesting new participant. This would indeed be happy news to share at work on Monday.

Since the mill was such a late entry, the committee had asked that we drive over and complete the necessary paperwork that afternoon. Nick, Casey and I got into my car and we drove to Coopers Mills where we met with one of the committee members in the town hall parking lot. I completed the necessary paperwork and paid the entrance fee.

Afterward, Nicholas treated me to an early supper at a restaurant in town. Later, we sat on the steps of the light tower, watching the sun go down and listening to the sounds of the ocean. The beauty of the sky and the setting sun helped to calm me. I was happy that my idea for the mill would bring joy to the mill employees, especially after the tragedy they had just endured. But I knew that I must keep working toward solving the mystery that was unfolding around me.

CHAPTER

Fourteen

I awoke on Sunday feeling a mixture of emotions. It was my birthday, which in itself conjured up all sorts of feelings. I was looking forward to church and my celebratory meal with my Uncle and cousins. As excited as I was for that, I could not shake the feeling of foreboding I had due, I believed to the death at the mill. And although I knew absolutely nothing about the players and the issues, I had a nagging feeling that the man's death had something to do with the missing hollow logs.

When I thought about it, it seemed absurd – how could there be any significance to some missing logs. And yet, I felt certain that somehow, they were a piece of a bigger mystery. I forced myself to concentrate on the mill's inclusion in the upcoming festival – I hoped it would bring some light where there was darkness.

Nicholas and I rose early, ate a light breakfast and headed for church services with Casey in tow. As we arrived at church, we caught sight of my Uncle and cousins just getting out of their car. We greeted them warmly and then headed for the church building. Suddenly, I caught sight of Ian and his children. About the same time, they had noticed me. I motioned for my group to pause and I went straight over to Ian.

"Good morning Ian!" I said. "I didn't know you attended services here."

"Good morning Holly," Ian said in return. "We are attending here today because it's close to my brother's farm. We are visiting there after services."

"I am here with my Uncle and cousins and they run a farm nearby too," I said. "Come, I'd love to introduce you."

At this, Brian who had been patiently standing by looked slightly annoyed. Sandy and Sheila took their father's arms and they began to follow me.

"Uncle Silas," I started, "may I introduce Ian Mckittrick and his son Brian and daughters Sandy and Sheila."

My Uncle and Ian exchanged a warm greeting.

"Brian, Sandy and Sheila, may I introduce my cousins Abigail, Aaron and Nathaniel," I finished. At this I couldn't help but notice a definitive shift in the air. The group exchanged kind pleasantries but then my cousins and Ian's children stood staring at each another. It was obvious to me at once that there was some kind of chemistry passing between the boys and girls and I suddenly felt like a matchmaker.

Nicholas noticed it to and rescued the moment from awkwardness by announcing that we had better move inside and take our seats. Once inside, we seated ourselves in a pew behind Ian's family.

Nicholas leaned over and whispered in my ear, "This

is certainly an interesting dynamic, isn't it?" he asked with a smile.

"You noticed it too?" I responded. "They all seem star-struck!"

"There is definitely something in the air," he agreed.

As the service moved along, my mind wandered onto the events of the week and now the chance meeting with Ian and his family. Before I knew it, Ian's family was turning around to share the sign of peace. As Ian's children and my cousins exchanged hands, the air was filled with a muted excitement. It was obvious to me that this group was attracted to each other.

After the recessional, we made our way slowly outside. It was a cold but sunny day. To my surprise, my Uncle turned to Ian and invited him and his children to come back to the farm to join in my birthday dinner.

"I thank you very much," Ian replied to the invitation, "but we are expected at my brother's house for dinner today. I hope that we could come another time. And we wish you a happy birthday Holly."

My Uncle said yes, of course, the offer was open-ended. After saying our goodbyes, we parted ways. My cousins were silent.

"Well," I said, "they are a nice family, aren't they? And none of Ian's children are…are attached."

At this I received a barrage of embarrassed protestations from my cousins. My Uncle and Nicholas burst into laughter. When we had settled down, we made our customary visit to my mother's grave, but on this day, it also felt like a way to include her in the birthday festivities.

"Alright everyone," Nicholas said, "we will follow you back to the farm."

At the farm, Nicholas, Casey and I spent hours enjoying a delicious meal and a leisurely stroll around the farm. In the late afternoon, after the weather had turned colder, we sat around a firepit enjoying warm cider. As I sat there, I took in the scene with a very full heart. I had always longed to belong somewhere and here I was, enjoying my birthday for the first time in my life, with family. There was no greater gift on Earth than being able to watch them talking and laughing, enjoying each other's company. Even the dogs seemed very content.

I didn't want the night to end but Nicholas said it must as it was dark and time to be starting for the lighthouse. My Uncle and cousins begged us to stay the night saying they had more than enough room. I looked at Nick and he agreed it would be okay. I thanked him later for giving me the best birthday gift of all – being able to wake up in a house full of family! We waited until the fire had gone out and then said our goodnights. Abby showed us each to spare guest rooms. The next morning I awoke to the fabulous smell of home-cooked breakfast. Nick and I shared another wonderful meal with my Uncle and cousins and then, after thanking them profusely for their hospitality, we reluctantly said our goodbyes and started out for the lighthouse.

On the way, Nicholas suggested we go into town and see if the sheriff had any updates on the death at the mill. He also suggested that we might stop in and see Dr. Thomas if he was available. I agreed to the plans and my cousin skillfully navigated the car to the sheriff's station, which wasn't far from the town center in Coopers Mills.

The building was bigger than I expected and there were a few police vehicles in the parking lot. We parked the car, leaving Casey in it with the windows down. We entered the building and asked to see the sheriff. Within moments, the sheriff came to greet us.

"Good morning Nick and Miss Snow," he said. "How are you this morning?"

"We're doing well Adam, thank you," my cousin responded. "We are wondering if you have any news about Mike Carter," he continued, as the sheriff ushered us into a nearby meeting room.

"We have been through his place," the sheriff started, "and his bank account. We found one large cash deposit, made very recently. We have questioned his parents. They knew he worked at the mill and were unaware of any other job. They don't know how he might have come by that sum of money."

"A large cash deposit," Nicholas repeated. "That sounds like some kind of payoff. But just what could he have been involved in?"

"We will be questioning some of his friends to see if we can get any clue as to what he was up to," the sheriff said. "I will keep you informed."

"Thank you Sheriff Dineen," I said, "and if we come across anything, we will be sure to let you know."

We bade the sheriff goodbye, got into the car and headed for Dr. Thomas' house.

"That large deposit certainly seems suspicious, doesn't it?" I asked my cousin.

"Clearly the man was involved in something," Nick answered.

"You don't really think the mill is mixed up in this, do you?" I asked.

My cousin didn't answer right away and appeared to be searching for the right words to answer with.

"I hope not Holly," was all he said.

Dr. Thomas was between appointments and received us enthusiastically. He wanted to know all about my telepathic experiences to date and launched into an interesting albeit lengthy monologue on the origins and history of telepathy. He said that I might benefit from joining in one or two sessions of a small group of telepaths that met at the hospital once a month. He was observing them and collecting data for a research paper he was doing on the subject.

After agreeing to visit his group, Nick and I made our exit and headed back to the lighthouse.

CHAPTER

Fifteen

The weeks following the death of the mill employee were somewhat dismal ones.

Staff at the mill seemed anxious at times. One thing keeping spirits up was the mill's participation in the festival. The employees who had volunteered to run games and show off their work seemed grateful to have this to plan for and look forward to. I was very glad the idea had been well received by everyone.

The more I thought about it, the more convinced I was that the missing hollow logs had something to do with the death at the mill, although I couldn't work out the connection. Slowly and nonchalantly, I made inquiries with Sandy and Sheila about the lumber. Eventually I learned that every part of a tree was used for something, even hollow logs which I learned were one of nature's anomalies. It seemed that even they could be ground into sawdust which had many uses such as bedding, stove pellets and edging for around plant beds.

In my studies of the mill, I learned that the hollow logs were indeed kept in a certain location and I was determined to keep my eye on that pile. One day while I was in town picking up sandwiches for lunch, I was chatting generally with the clerk at the counter.

"Oh, you're from the mill," she said. "The McKittricks are legendary around these parts for how hard they work and what a beautiful product they turn out!" I thanked her for the high praise and she continued.

"They must run themselves ragged working there day and night. I don't live too far from the mill and I know they work many nights, although we really appreciate that they don't turn on the big lights so folks around here are not disturbed."

I hadn't the least idea about what she was saying but I merely thanked her, collected my packages and left the store. On the short walk back to the mill, my mind was filled with questions. Sandy and Sheila were eagerly awaiting my return. Lunch time often consisted of our eating right in the office as customers could come in anytime. While we ate our sandwiches, I casually asked the girls about overtime and late night work at the mill.

"Oh, father is very strict about that," Sheila said. "Once in a great while if we have a large rush order he might have some of the men working later but it's rare. Generally we are finished for the day by seven and that's everything, workers and Brian with the books."

Her answer was what I had expected, so then who was putting in late nights at the mill and why? I decided that some reconnaissance was in order. On a break, I telephoned Nicholas to tell him what I had learned, but was only able to leave the information in a voice message for him. Hopefully he would agree that something was up and that watching the mill might be a good idea.

In addition to spending time with the girls in the office, I spent a couple of hours looking at the books with Brian. He was cordial enough and spent, I thought, a generous amount of time with me describing how the accounts worked and how the mill made its profit. I enjoyed being at the mill every day and the more I learned, the more I wanted to know.

This particular night, I left work around five-thirty in the evening. The ride home to the lighthouse only took about twenty-five minutes. Suddenly along the way I was forced to pull the car over to the side of the road. A horrible feeling of anxiety and despair came over me. Casey must have sensed my upset because he joined me in the front seat trying to console me. I sat collecting myself for a few minutes and then started out again. I couldn't imagine what had come over me.

When I reached the lighthouse, it was dark and Nicholas' car wasn't there but I was not overly concerned about its absence. Casey and I exited the car and made our way to the front door. Once inside, a cold chill swept over me. I did not feel the happy, warm feeling I usually had when I entered the house. I turned lights on as I made my way to the den. As I approached the desk, I could see a note with my name on it.

Holly, had to return to New York for a series of meetings. Should be back late this evening. Nick.

I emptied my mind and tried to call out to Nicholas but no response came. I lit the fireplace in the living room and decided to start dinner, assuring myself that my cousin would no doubt get in touch with me. Casey laid down in front of the fire while I moved toward the kitchen. As I gathered ingredients for dinner, there was a knock at the door. I opened it to find Sheriff Dineen and Mr. Manning on my doorstep.

"Oh, Mr. Manning, I didn't know that you were in town. Hello Sheriff Dineen, please come in," I said as I stepped back to let them enter. Both men stepped into the foyer but neither spoke. I was about to offer them seats but the look on their faces scared me.

"What is it?" I asked sharply. "What is wrong?"

"Holly," Mr. Manning began, "Nicholas was to fly to New York for meetings today. The helicopter he was riding in went down in the Adirondacks."

I went completely numb. All I could do was stare at them.

"The area is quite remote," the sheriff said, "and at the moment, the team in the air has spotted the debris field but the search and rescue team on the ground can't get near it because of the terrain and the weather."

"Debris field?" I asked weakly.

"Don't panic Holly," begged Mr. Manning leading me into the living room and depositing me into a chair. "We don't know anything for sure at this point. Nicholas is strong. The terrain is tough but when the weather breaks they will call in a special team that can repel into the area."

I sat there thinking about Nicholas. I just couldn't have lost him. I repeated his name over and over again in my mind hoping that he would answer but there was no reply.

"Is there someone we can call for you?" the sheriff was asking.

"Would you please call my Uncle Silas?" I answered. "I will get you the number. Mr. Manning, would you, could you stay the night? It's too late for you to go back to New York. There is plenty of room here and I would be so grateful to have your company."

"Thank you Holly," the lawyer said gently, "I would be happy to stay. I will go and put some coffee on."

After giving the Sheriff my uncle's telephone number, I sank back down into a chair. Casey sat right next to me, as if sensing exactly what was going on. The sheriff went through to the kitchen to make the call. I could hear him telling my uncle what was known so far, that I had invited Mr. Manning to stay and that I seemed to be holding up. The sheriff finished the call and came back through to the living room just as Mr. Manning was pouring the coffee.

"Your uncle is very upset and is glad you will not be alone tonight," the sheriff reported. "He and his children will call on you tomorrow. He suggested that going forward, his boys take turns staying here at night with you."

"Thank you Sheriff Dineen, for everything," I said. "You will keep us updated?"

"Yes of course Miss Snow," he replied. He declined to stay for coffee saying he must get back to his office.

After the sheriff left, Mr. Manning and I sat quietly, sipping our coffee. All at once I said, "It wasn't a car accident, but it was another accident."

Mr. Manning's head came up quickly and his eyes met mine.

"Yet another important person in my life involved in an accident. And what do you make of this…." I launched into the story about the missing hollow logs, the death at the mill and the lights seen at the mill after hours. "I am sure something is going on and I mean to get to the bottom of it. I was going to suggest to Nick that we start staking out the place at night."

For a moment I thought he was going to tell me I was crazy. Instead he agreed with everything I said and proposed that he stay on with me at the lighthouse instead of asking my cousins to do it. They were needed at the farm and he could watch over me just as well and he added, he could do his work from anywhere. I thought about his offer and readily agreed.

The days that followed the news of Nicholas' death were a blur. Uncle Silas and his family came to see me, Gerard called Ian and informed him of the news and said I would be taking a few days off. The sheriff came to visit me and relay the news that from what the search party could see, there had been no survivors. It appeared that weather had caused the accident. Even Max and his mother made an appearance, having heard the news as it circulated through the company. Max did seem truly sorry for my loss and even hugged me, saying that I must call on him if I should need anything. Margaret didn't hug me but did say she was sorry for my loss.

Two weeks after Nicholas' death, I found myself restless and deeply anxious wondering how I could go on without him. I would work at the mill during the day and return to the lighthouse at night. I believe I would have gone mad if Gerard Manning hadn't been there with me. He had insisted on staying. He did his work, cooked for us and was a very pleasant companion. He was a quiet strength in my days.

On the Monday evening before the town festival in Coopers Mills, as Gerard read the paper in the living room with Casey, I ventured up into the attic and stared at scores of boxes. As I started examining the ones closest to the attic opening, I discovered a box with the word 'Journals' written on it. I carried it downstairs to the living room where Gerard looked up from his paper to observe what I was doing, but didn't say a word.

I sat down in a chair across from Gerard in front of the roaring fireplace and set the box on the floor next to me. I opened it and found it filled with books. I picked one up and opened it. I recognized my mother's handwriting. As I turned the pages, I caught sight of an entry dated a few months before her death. As I read the passage, a growing apprehension overtook me. My mother had seen a figure lurking around the lighthouse too. And she had apparently been friends with Ian McKittrick, who had mentioned some strange goings on at the mill, while Max was in charge, including several visits from Margaret Rothchilde and at odd hours of the day.

I shared what I had read with Gerard and told him of my belief that my parents' deaths and all the accidents were somehow connected with the mill, although I couldn't work out how. I was determined to find the answer and I suggested that we start poking around the mill at night after everyone had left.

"Why not start tonight?" I asked. "We can go by boat or by car."

I had expected Gerard to vehemently protest, but to my surprise, he agreed almost instantly. We decided to take the car and after leaving lights on to make the house look like we were at home, we locked the door behind us. Quietly, with Casey at our heels, we made our way to the car and started off. It was around eight o'clock and we didn't pass another car on the road to the mill.

When we reached the long driveway that lead to the mill, we parked the car just off the main road and continued on foot. I had brought Casey's leash so I could keep him close to us. We stayed near the tree line and several times stopped just to listen. Casey listened too, but did not appear to be bothered by anything. The only sound we heard was the sound of the water rushing over the falls. The mill appeared deserted. It was a cold night, but there was no wind. A cloudless sky and a three-quarter moon illuminated the sky just enough for us to see without using flashlights. We stayed hidden from sight behind some palates of wood. After almost half an hour, Gerard motioned for me to follow him back to the car.

On the ride home, we tried to work out various theories about what could be going on at the mill. As we clearly didn't have enough information to work with, we formed no conclusions. Gerard wanted me to promise not to go to the mill without him and I reluctantly agreed. Back at the house, he said good night and I stayed up long into the night tending the fire and reading from my mother's journals. I sat in the chair by the fire in the den reading. Every once in a while my mind wandered and I found myself thinking of Nicholas. How I ached to see him and hear his voice. I closed my mind and focused on him.

Holly.

I opened my eyes with a start. Some sudden whim made me run through to the living room and look out the front window, Casey at my heels. I strained my eyes trying to see through the dark night. I could just make out someone standing at the mouth of the driveway. The dog seemed to sense it too but much to my surprise, he didn't bark or act upset. I reached down to pat the dog and when I looked up again the figure had gone. I wondered if I had imagined the whole thing. Eventually, I put out all the lights and Casey and I made our way upstairs to bed.

CHAPTER
Sixteen

The next morning I mentioned what had happened to Gerard. I also mentioned that during the night it occurred to me that we should make sure the light tower was secure and that no one had broken into it. I thought it would be a good chance for me to really check out the tower as I had not taken an opportunity to do that since I arrived. Gerard offered to do it for me. He said that Horace would be delivering groceries later that morning and that the two of them and Casey would give the tower a thorough going over. After a light breakfast, I bade my companions goodbye and headed off to work.

At the mill, I happened to notice that the pile of hollow logs had grown in size. I mentioned this to Sandy and Sheila who said that the hollow logs were a special order by a Mr. Smith a few towns away. He would order them a few times a year. The girls were not sure what he used them for but speculated that he was an artist and used them in his art work.

That evening I was determined to go back to the mill, but I decided to go late and alone. I waited for Gerard to retire to his room. When I felt certain that he was asleep, I crept quietly downstairs. Casey tried to come with me but I whispered in his ear that he must stay and protect the house. He reluctantly let me go and once outside, I debated about whether to take the car or the boat. The boat would be faster and I was afraid that Gerard might hear the car motor start up.

Again, it was cloudless sky and the moon was bright so I was able to follow the path down to the beach fairly easily. I moved swiftly along the dock and climbed into the boat. I started the engine and moved along slowly, staying close to the shoreline. On the first trip with Nicholas in the boat, I had taken notice of a dock not far from the mill, but out of sight of it. I decided I would leave the boat there and continue on foot toward the mill. I carefully navigated the boat alongside of the dock, cut the motor and secured the mooring line.

I hurried along the dock and discovered a path that led in the direction of the mill. I followed it and soon came out on a hill overlooking the mill on the opposite side of the water from the mill. I had never noticed it before, but there was a footbridge across the water that passed closely by the waterwheel. As I was about to move forward onto the bridge, a movement below caught my eye. I could see a figure wading in the water where the logs were corralled before they were moved out to sea.

I moved back into the trees and watched as the figure seemed to be moving logs around. It was too dark to see exactly what was going on. Suddenly the figure moved to shore and headed for the mill and I could see that it was carrying something. Quickly and quietly I started across the footbridge and toward a door that was nearby the waterwheel. On the other side, I removed my key ring from my pocket and tried couple of keys before I found the right one and let myself in. I was upstairs in the mill looking down on the floor. The mill was silent and dark and for a moment I thought about turning around and getting away.

I heard soft movement below me and it seemed to ignite my fury that someone was sneaking around my mill. I summoned up all of my courage and moved toward the stairs. I crept down them as quietly as I could. As I reached the lower platform, I stopped to listen for the intruder. All at once, I heard a sound behind me and suddenly I was being held firm against someone. I struggled and fought, causing my attacker to lose footing and fall with me in his arms. As we fell, I rolled away grabbing the flashlight out of my pocket and turning it on.

"Brian!" I exclaimed.

"Holly!" he exclaimed in return.

We stood up looking at each other in disbelief.

"What are you doing here in the middle of the night?" I demanded.

"What am I doing here? What are you doing here?" he asked, looking at me as though trying to size me up. "Come with me," he demanded suddenly.

I made no move to follow him, not sure what to make of him.

"I won't hurt you," he said calmly. "We need to talk."

He moved toward the stairs and started up. I followed cautiously and he led the way into one of the meeting rooms. Instead of turning on the lights, he lit a candle and then made sure the window shades were down. I took a seat at the table while he removed his boots and waterproof overalls, which he hung over a chair. Then he stepped back into his boots and took a seat facing me. I wasn't sure what to think, but I wasn't feeling any sense of danger from him.

"I didn't hurt you just now, did I?" he asked.

"No," I answered. "I'm okay. Listen, I feel like something is going on here at the mill. I don't know what but I've decided that as its owner, I have to investigate."

"I couldn't agree with you more," Brian said. "Something is going on here. I've been suspicious for some time so I've started coming here to investigate too."

"Does it have something to do with hollow logs?" I asked.

He looked surprised at my question and took a moment before speaking.

"Come downstairs, there's something you should see," he answered, blowing out the candle.

Slowly and quietly we moved to the first floor platform and made our way into the store front. Here again, he lit a candle and pointed to the counter where a log, still wet, was laying.

"I fished this out of the corral tonight," Brian explained. "Just look at this."

As he spoke, he picked up a screwdriver and pried open a piece of the log which looked like a lid. He put the screwdriver down and moved the candle closer so that I could see inside. There was a small cavity in the hollowed out center of the log which contained a box. I looked at Brian who nodded as if indicating that I should remove the box. With trembling fingers, I reached in to retrieve it and found that the box was wedged into the center of the hollow log by two pieces of precisely cut styrofoam. Once these were removed I was able to take out the box. I set it on the counter and opened it. The box was filled with money and jewelry.

"What is going on here?" I cried, looking at Brian.

"I don't have the answers yet," he responded. "But I'll tell you this isn't the first log like this I've found. Someone is using hollow logs to move money and other items and they are using our mill to do it. Just two weeks ago, Tom O'Donnell's boy brought in a hollow log he found washed up two miles south of here. Tom brought it to me because it too contained a box of money. Tom thought maybe we had custom made it that way for a client and that somehow the log got washed away by mistake."

My mind was quickly trying to take in what Brian had told me.

"You think there are more like this in the corral right now?" I asked.

"I would bet on it," Brian answered.

"Brian, do you think Mike Carter could have made this same discovery?" I asked. "Do you think that's why he was killed?"

"I'm starting to believe this had something to do with it," Brian responded.

At this, I told Brian about overhearing Mike Carter express his concern about missing hollow logs in conversations with his co-workers.

"Apparently, he was on to something," I continued. "Maybe he got too close to the answer. We have got to investigate this but how? What if someone at the mill is involved?"

Brian started to answer and then stopped himself.

"Listen," Brian said, "it's very late. Let's get out of here and go home. Did you drive here?"

"No, I came by boat," I answered.

Brian raised an eyebrow and smiled.

"Wow, you are a brave and resourceful girl," he commented.

"Thanks," I said, somewhat embarrassed. "Let's slip out of here and go our separate ways. We will have to put our heads together and make our plan."

Brian said he would go out the office door and lock it behind him. I signaled that I would go back upstairs and out the door by the waterwheel, locking it behind me. I watched Brian go and then made my way slowly up the stairs and towards the door. I passed through the door, locking it after me. As I turned around to move toward the footbridge, I saw a figure standing on the other side. For a moment, I panicked realizing that Brian was probably already gone. The figure turned and ran away quickly into the woods.

For a moment I was tempted to race after the person. After rethinking that idea, I realized my priority was to reach the boat safely and get back to the lighthouse. Cautiously I made my way back to the dock, slipped into the boat and motored back toward the lighthouse. Ten minutes later saw me docking and making my way up the cliff path. I entered the house quietly and found Casey waiting for me in the living room. Once upstairs and tucked into bed, I let the night's events play over and over in my mind until sleep came.

I had been hopeful that Gerard was not aware of my activities the night before and from his conversation at breakfast, I felt certain he knew nothing. After wishing him a good day, I left for work. I arrived at the mill to find the girls in the office and Brian on the floor assisting with the cutting of a special order.

After lunch, I told Sheila and Sandy that I was going to work with Brian on the books. I found him outside, watching over the process of moving the logs in the corral out to sea where tugboats would move them south.

"I almost hate to move them," Brian confided in me as we moved inside and up to his office. "I'm sure there is more to discover there."

"You think there are more hollow logs stuffed with treasure?" I asked.

"I'm sure of it," he answered.

"Why not call Sheriff Dineen now and let him examine the logs before they're moved?" I suggested.

"No, we still don't have enough to go to the sheriff," Brian answered. "Here," he said pulling a book from his desk. "I have started keeping a log of my visits to the mill at night. I've been recording when I come and if I see activity and when I've found a hollow log with something inside. We need more of this information and if we can get any identifying marks off the boat that sometimes ties up at the dock at night that will help the sheriff too. I just don't want to scare off whoever is behind this."

"This is dangerous Brian," I said worried. "I'll agree that we can continue surveillance for a little while longer, but then we are going to have to go the sheriff."

With that decided, Brian also confided in me that he had purchased a book on forensic accounting to try to help him understand the entries in the mill books that he couldn't figure out. He said that he had come to realize that he had done as much as he could and that we would need more help and resources to follow the money trail.

On the way home that evening, I decided to tell Gerard everything that had happened. He and Casey were at the door to greet me and as soon as I was inside, I asked him to sit down in the living room where I recounted my trip to the mill, my encounter with Brian and all the details he had told me. Gerard listened attentively and after I had laid out all the details, I asked for his advice.

"You and Brian have done some excellent sleuthing," Gerard said. "But you are right. This can't go on much longer without involving the sheriff. Whoever is behind this is very dangerous Holly. I'm sure I can help Brian with the forensic accounting piece. Now dinner is waiting."

With that, Gerard led the way to the kitchen where we enjoyed his home cooked dinner. While he talked on about some of the recent work he was doing, I found myself surprised that he hadn't insisted that Brian and I stop our investigation at once and hand it over to the sheriff. I wondered what Nick would say. After dinner as I cleared away and washed the dishes, I forced myself to think about the upcoming weekend.

CHAPTER

Seventeen

The weekend of the fall festival was upon us and Coopers Mills was bustling in preparation. Town workers were busy cleaning up the grounds and the gazebo. It seemed that the festival was a real highlight of the season and was the start of months of celebrating with Thanksgiving and Christmas not far behind. Horace Cunningham had told me that some of the women who worked at the town hall spent their lunch hours decorating the gazebo, even the town clock and the surrounding grounds for the holidays and really went all out. And after the holidays, the little town would settle down quietly for the winter and come back to life in May or June once the snow had melted.

I didn't know how I would survive the holidays without Nicholas and was glad that I had the festival as a distraction. Employees at the mill were very excited about the weekend and eagerly looking forward to participating in the festival. Abby and I had worked at a feverish pace to finish her quilt and were eagerly looking forward to the weekend's activities. It was decided that Abby would stay at the lighthouse with me on Thursday night since it was closer to the town square than her family farm. That way on Friday morning, we could head to the church were the quilts would be displayed and judged and get set up. Aaron and Nathaniel would meet us there.

After work on Thursday, I headed straight for the lighthouse. I had gotten into the habit of leaving Casey with Gerard so that he would have company during the day, and protection if needed. It was dark when I arrived home because of the time of year, but I could see Abby's car parked on the point.

Gerard, Casey, Abby and Miss Molly greeted me at the door. I felt so happy to come home to a house full of people. The moment would have been magnificent if Nicholas had been standing there with them. I forced myself to push down the sadness and despair I felt from losing him and put a smile on my face as I greeted them and went inside. The aroma of home cooking greeted my nostrils as I entered the house and Abby told me that Gerard had prepared a full turkey dinner in honor of our big weekend.

"Oh Gerard," I exclaimed, "how kind of you. It smells wonderful!"

"Thank you Holly," he answered smiling proudly. "I really learned to cook after my wife died. It was that or eat in restaurants for the rest of my life. I actually do enjoy it. I find it relieves the stress of the day."

Abby had set the table and had gone into the yard to clip some greens and berries to decorate the table. Suddenly we heard her scream. Gerard and I, along with the dogs, rushed into the yard looking for her.

We saw her near the trees where the driveway emptied onto the point.

"What is it Abby?" I called as we ran toward her.

"I saw someone moving in the trees," she answered, moving toward us.

I didn't hesitate. I ran strait toward the hollowed out tree, determined to finally catch the mysterious figure. Casey and Miss Molly were at my heels barking wildly.

"No Holly!" I heard Gerard yell behind me.

All at once I heard a snapping sound, felt excruciating pain in my left leg and fell to the ground.

Abby and Gerard were by my side in seconds. The dogs ran into the woods.

"What is it?" I gasped, almost blacking out from pain.

"It's some king of trap," Gerard answered grimly. "Abby see if you can find a stick or something to pry it open with. Hurry!"

"I'll get the poker from the fireplace," she said as she sprinted toward the house.

"Hold on Holly," Gerard coaxed me. The dogs returned from the woods and stayed close as Abby ran back to us with the poker in hand. Gerard used it to pry open the trap and release my ankle.

"Thank heavens you were wearing pants and boots or this could have been much worse," Gerard said as he and Abby helped me to stand.

Then, with one of them on each side of me, they helped and half carried me to the house with the dogs at our heels. They took me straight into the kitchen where Abby removed my boot and took scissors to my pant leg. In no time, she had the grisly wound exposed. If the sight of blood bothered either one of them, they showed no sign of it.

Gerard called the doctor and the sheriff while Abby carefully cleaned the wound. About twenty-five minutes later saw both the doctor and the sheriff present. Dr. Thomas agreed with Gerard, that it could have been much worse. Even still, I would need a few stitches. The doctor praised Abby for the work she had done to expose and clean the wound.

Abby shyly explained that she had vast experience with wounds from tending to her farm animals and her brothers. As the doctor prepared for my light surgery, Sheriff Dineen re-entered saying that I had been very lucky. The trap was old and the spring mechanism was not really working properly. The sheriff said he would take the trap along with him and see if they could retrieve any fingerprints off of it. Abby had been busy preparing me a make-shift bed out of one of the couches in the living room so that I would not have to try to manage the stairs.

After being stitched up, I was deposited on the couch. Dr. Thomas gave me a tetanus shot and left pain medication, saying that the wound should heal nicely but would hurt for a few days. I should expect bruising and throbbing pain, the doctor advised, but if I should develop a fever, I was to phone him immediately. We would make a plan for me to go to him or him to come back to the lighthouse to remove the stiches in a few days.

After the doctor left I said, "Well I've certainly ruined dinner."

"Holly, don't worry about that," Gerard said. "The important thing is that you are going to be alright."

"If you feel up to eating something Holly, I can bring you some food," Abby offered.

I didn't want to disappoint either of them as they had both been through as awful an ordeal as I had.

I agreed to eat. Abby made plates of food for all of us and we ate together in the living room while discussing the night's events.

"Obviously someone put that trap there deliberately," I said. "Nicholas and I had discovered the hollowed out tree and suspected that someone has been using it to keep watch on the lighthouse."

"Who would do such a thing?" Abby asked.

"I wish we could discover that," Gerard answered. "It may explain a number of things."

"Abby," I said, "this isn't going to change anything for tomorrow. I am still going with you to help set up the quilt…"

"Oh no," Abby replied. "I wouldn't dream of making you hobble around."

"Please Abby," I begged. "I don't want to miss this."

"I have it!" Gerard exclaimed. "Let's call the boys. I'm sure they would love to help."

"Yes," Abby agreed, "what a wonderful idea."

As she went to the kitchen to phone her brothers, I looked at Gerard.

"Thank heavens it was me and not either of you who stepped into that trap," I said.

"I can't shake the feeling that whoever has done this is responsible for all the accidents in the family," Gerard said slowly and deliberately. "I am gravely concerned about what might happen next."

I shuddered at his words, realizing that whoever was behind what was going on must be very desperate to go to such lengths. My heart ached for Nicholas. I wished he was here. And like Gerard, I too was worried about what was still to come.

Abby returned saying that her family was shocked at

the news of my accident. The boys were on their way to the lighthouse and her father had insisted that one or the other of them remain with us at the lighthouse until we were certain that any danger had passed.

"Oh I couldn't ask them to do that," I protested. "What about your farm and all of your responsibilities? After tonight you will be back home safely Abby so there will be no need for your brothers to stay here."

"Oh yes they will stay," Abby said firmly. "We have only just found you Holly and we are not letting some mad man take you away from us."

I looked at her and Gerard. A feeling of warmth rose up in me almost bringing tears to my eyes. The depth of Abby's love and her fearless courage in the face of clear danger made me feel gratitude and admiration for her. Although I had no idea of what the danger was, I felt myself extremely fortunate to be facing it with such a wonderful group of people. The three of us sat by the fire with the dogs awaiting the arrival of the boys.

After some time, the dogs became restless and then started barking as a car drove onto the point. Abby went to the window and then announced the boys had arrived.

She opened the door and she and the dogs went out to greet them.

Once inside, Aaron and Nathaniel came to me and each in turn knelt down to embrace me. I thanked them for coming and told them how safe they made me feel. Abby then took charge, asking the boys to bring their overnight bags and follow her upstairs, explaining to them as they went that they would occupy the room across from Gerard's. There was one bed so for tonight one of them would take the bed and the other be in the sleeping bag on the floor. I noticed Gerard watching the scene unfold with a warm and satisfied look on his face.

"Gerard," I said wearily, "thank you so much for finding me and giving me a family."

He looked at me and said very gently, "You're welcome my dear. Now, it's time for you to get some sleep. I will be right here."

I reached out for his hand. He took my hand and held it tight. He helped me to get comfortable on my pillow and covered me with a blanket. I was asleep in seconds.

On Friday morning, I awoke to the fabulous aroma of bacon and coffee and I could hear that people were moving around in the kitchen. I sat up and was attempting to get up when Nathaniel came out of the kitchen to help me. He helped to steady me and then retrieved an intricately carved walking stick that had been placed by the couch. He explained that it had been made by his father who had insisted that it was brought along for me to use. I tried it out and found that it was a tremendous help toward allowing me to walk with only a slight limp.

I joined others in the kitchen and we sat at the table enjoying Abby's breakfast. It made me happy to have a house full of people. After breakfast, it was decided that Gerard and Casey would drive to town and check in with the sheriff while the rest of us and Miss Molly would drive to Coopers Mills to get Abby set up.

After several trips back and forth to the house, the cars were loaded and we were ready to set off. Abby drove my car while the boys followed in their truck. Although it was still early when we arrived, the town square was already very busy. People were setting up display tables and tents. I made Abby drive slowly and honk the horn as we passed by the spot where employees from the mill were setting up games and displays. I waved at them as we drove by.

Abby continued on toward the little church and parked on the street. The boys parked the truck in the church lot to be nearer a door. They began to unload items from the truck bed and move them into the church. Abby took the quilt from the car and headed toward the door. I limped along behind her with Miss Molly at my side. Although she was Abby's dog, she seemed to know that I was injured and had decided I needed looking after.

I noticed that Abby had stopped to speak to a group of people. As I got closer, I saw that it was Brian and his sisters. I remembered that the girls were entering a quilt too and I suddenly wondered how I would explain my injury. I decided that I would be careful about how much I said to the girls. I would try to find a moment alone with Brian to fill him in on the details.

By the time I had reached where they were standing, Brian, Sheila and Sandy had all noticed that I was limping and using a cane.

"What has happened?" Sheila cried, as she and Sandy came to my side.

"Oh, I'm fine really," I answered, shooting a warning look at Abby, "I was hiking on the cliff trail last evening and I fell and cut my leg. Really, it's nothing serious at all."

"Yes," Abby added understanding my warning glance. "I was with her. It was really the dogs - they made her trip."

Sheila and Sandy seemed to accept the explanation,

but I could tell that Brian was immediately suspicious. He said nothing but I could see he was deep in thought. I caught his eye and we exchanged a knowing glance. I limped along toward the door with Sheila and Sandy at my side, while Brian walked along with Abby. I could see by his body language that he was definitely smitten with Abby.

When we entered the church, I saw Aaron and Nathaniel hard at work assembling the wooden frame from which Abby's quilt would hang. While the boys worked on that, Abby began to put some decorative pumpkins and gourds near the frame. I shifted my attention from Abby and her brothers, to Brian and his sisters. Brian was hard at work helping them but more than once I caught him looking over at Abby. Brian left the girls for a while to go and help employees from the mill set up the log rolling and log cutting contests. Ian had stayed back at the mill with staff so that the mill could honor its usual Friday business hours.

At last the moment came to hang the quilt. Abby carefully removed it from a bag and gave it to the boys to hold while she used clothes pins to attach it to the frame. I noticed that several women in the room, including Sandy and Sheila, had stopped their work and were waiting for a look at Abby's quilt. At last it was attached to the frame and the frame was raised into position. We stepped back to look at it. I could actually hear some sighs of admiration in the room and even I was mesmerized by looking at it. Of course I had seen it before, but there was something sensational about seeing it hanging there – its beauty was inspiring.

Abby had named the quilt 'Holly's Storm at Sea' for which I was deeply flattered and somehow, the name was strangely reflective of all that was going on in my life.

The quilt was large, eighty-six inches by eighty-six inches and it only contained three colors – dark blue, light blue and white. The pattern went from top to bottom and side to side, a square within a square, making it seem endless just like the sea. Although it contained only three colors, the juxtaposition of the light and dark colors made it a feast for the eye. It was dramatic and it was obvious that the assembly of the pattern required pinpoint accuracy. I thought back on all of the ironing and starching of fabric that we had done and of all of the machine and hand sewing that Abby had done. The end result was exquisite.

All at once I heard Abby exclaim, "Oh no!"

"What is it Abby?" I asked, limping closer to her.

"I can't find the hang tag," she said, looking frantically around her. "It identifies me and the quilt. Every quilt must have one."

Suddenly in my mind's eye, I could see the hang tag laying on my desk in the den at the lighthouse.

"Oh Abby," I cried. "This is my fault. After I wrote out the tag, I left it on my desk at the lighthouse."

"We'll go for it sis," the boys offered.

"No, thank you," she said. "You stay here and set up the cornstalks and hay bales. I promised the decorating committee that we would put them around the room. They are too heavy for us to bring in. Holly, may I borrow your car?"

"Yes, of course," I answered, handing her the car key. "I'll come with you."

"No, I'm not going to make you limp all over," she

said. "I will be alright. I'm just going to run in and out of the lighthouse. I'll be back soon."

And with that she ran off with Miss Molly following closely behind her. While the boys worked to decorate the room, I slowly moved around watching as other women were setting up their quilts. I stopped near Sandy and Sheila's entry and complimented the girls on their quilt. While the girls continued their work, Brian and I moved away and I told him what had really happened to me the night before. He felt as I did, that we must be getting too close to exposing whatever was going on and my accident was a warning.

While we stood there talking, I had noticed a woman enter the church and start to walk around looking at the quilts. All at once, I realized that it was Margaret Rothchilde. I told Brian and asked him to follow me. We approached Margaret and when she recognized me, she stopped suddenly. Our eyes met. I was taken back by the wild, desperate look in her eyes.

"Mrs. Rothchilde," I said calmly, "can I help you?"

"Please," she said weakly, "You must go to make it stop."

After speaking, she appeared very unstable on her feet and Brian rushed forward and caught her. Aaron and Nathaniel had noticed the commotion and came over.

"Boys, see if you can find a doctor on the grounds," I commanded. They ran off at once to carry out their mission without asking any questions.

Brian had tenderly placed Margaret Rothchilde in a chair. I knelt down beside her and took her hand.

"Mrs. Rothchilde," I said, "please tell me what is worrying you."

"There is nothing more to say," came the answer. She said it with great force and seemed to come to life as she did it. She stood up, stumbling slightly. Brian reached out a hand to steady her, but she pushed him away.

"Go at once," she repeated and she slowly moved away.

I started after her but Brian put his hand on my arm.

"Let her go," he said. "She isn't worth it."

"What do you mean?" I asked, surprised at what he had said.

"She has a nasty reputation for getting what she wants at any cost," he stated. "At any cost."

As I was trying to process what Brian had said, we started to hear constant barking and suddenly, Miss Molly came running into the church. Although we waited, Abby did not appear. I began to think that Abby could not possibly have made it to the lighthouse and back. I wondered if maybe she hadn't gone at all. I mentioned this to Brian and we made our way outside to see if the car had returned. Aaron and Nathaniel joined us saying they couldn't find a doctor but that they had heard talk among the crowd that someone had crashed a car. The car had gone off the main road less than a mile from the festival site and had crashed into a ravine.

"Abby!" I exclaimed.

My heart sunk immediately and I could hear Gerard Manning's voice in my head saying that my parents had died in car accidents. I told the boys to get their car at once and follow us. Brian, Miss Molly and I got into his truck. The dog had stopped barking as if satisfied that we had understood her. When we arrived at the scene, the fire department was already there. I could see a few bystanders had gathered and were looking down into the ravine.

My heart practically stopped as I saw that it was indeed my car at the bottom, lodged among some trees.

Brian ran down the steep hill, half falling, followed by Abby's brothers. They assisted the fire department in retrieving Abby from the car. As I watched the scene unfold, I heard my name.

"Holly?" It was Max and he looked shocked to see me.

"Max, what are you doing here?" I asked.

"I thought you were in the car," he said, not answering my question.

At that moment, our attention was diverted by the scene below. Abby had been freed from the vehicle. Brian and her brothers were carrying her uphill on a stretcher toward a waiting ambulance.

As they came past us, I could hear Abby murmuring, "...my quilt, the quilt..." They placed her in the ambulance and it was agreed that her brothers and Miss Molly would follow the ambulance to the hospital in their truck and call their father to inform him about what had happened. Brian and I would go to the lighthouse and get the hang tag for the quilt. The judging of the quilting entries would be happening in less than two hours. I had to get to the lighthouse and back with the hang tag and I would have to stand in for Abby during the judging.

"What happened?" Max asked, still lingering at the scene. "Do they know what caused the accident?"

"At this point, no," Brian answered. "They will tow the car in to be inspected and hopefully Abigail can tell them what happened."

"I don't know anything about cars," Max responded. "I do hope she will be alright. Holly, can I give you a ride to the hospital?"

"Thank you Max," I said. "I am going to ride with Brian."

Although he smiled pleasantly at my refusal, I sensed that my brother was irritated with my decision. As we turned to leave the scene, we came face to face with Margaret Rothchilde.

"Mother, what are you doing here?" Max exclaimed.

Before we could hear her response, Max took her by the arm and led her away. I advised Brian that I wanted to speak with Sheriff Dineen before we left. When we found him, I asked him to take my car to the most reputable garage he knew to have it checked over thoroughly. I told him my suspicion that the crash had not been an accident. He wanted to know more but I begged him to let us finish that conversation later as we needed to finish getting Abby's quilt ready for the judging. He reluctantly agreed and said he would tow the car back to the sheriff's station where he'd have a specialist examine it. I agreed to phone him later.

"Where can I take you?" Brian asked as we headed toward his truck.

"First to the lighthouse to get the hang tag for Abby's quilt," I answered. "That's what she was on her way to retrieve when this happened."

"You really don't believe this was an accident?" Brian asked as we climbed into his truck and started off.

"Too many people in my life have had accidents, not to mention mine last night," I said, "I'm afraid Abby is the latest victim. I have to get to the bottom of whatever is going on here."

"Listen, I want to tell you something," Brian started, "and I should have told you this the other night at the mill. In the last months that Max was in charge there, I started to find accounting entries that I couldn't understand. When I questioned Max, he said that his mother and corporate headquarters had ordered the entries. He said it was some adjustment necessary as the result of some corporate audit. I accepted his answer at the time but I'm wondering if the Rothchildes are involved. The only problem with that theory is that they're rich, so I find it hard to believe that they would need to move cash and jewelry in hollow logs. Still, wasn't it creepy the way she turned up this morning?"

"Hollow logs and odd accounting entries," I said. "I feel like we are no closer to understanding what is going on," I said in an exasperated voice. "And yes, it was odd to see Margaret this morning. For people who live in New York, they certainly spend a lot of time here."

"Well, there's more," Brian continued. "Remember when I told you that I've been investigating myself? Well I've staked out the mill on several nights and several times I've seen a boat tie up to the mill dock and four or five people get off and go into the mill. They're real careful not to turn on too many lights or start up equipment. But they must be in there stuffing the hollow logs because I see them come down the water chute into the corral with the other logs. I've wanted to confront these people, but I feel there is something dangerous about the situation. Now maybe it's time we involve the sheriff."

I listened in fascinated horror as Brian continued his story.

"I have come to the conclusion that maybe they are placing a lumber order and before it's shipped, they stuff the hollow logs and put them in with the order so cash and jewelry can be moved without anyone knowing it. These have to be bad people doing this," he concluded.

"Brian," I said as the lighthouse came into view, "I believe you have hit on something and you're right that it's time to inform Sheriff Dineen and get his help. Stop here, I'm just going to run inside and grab the hang tag for the quilt and we can get back on the road,"

Brian parked and I got out and made my way as quickly as I could to the door. Once inside, I went straight to the desk in the den and picked up the hang tag. As I started out of the den, I caught sight of something in my peripheral vision. I went through the kitchen to look out the door and I saw the door to the light tower swinging open and shut in the breeze. I went outside at once to inform Brian, who decided we had better investigate.

With Brian in the lead, we cautiously approached the tower. I mentioned to Brian that since I had arrived there, I had never taken the time to explore the tower but that Gerard had done so recently. As we peered inside the door, we could see nothing amiss on the ground level. As we looked upward, we could see that stairs wound around and around toward the top. We could see a landing about halfway up and Brian signaled that we should investigate.

Brian was worried about my climbing the stairs with my injury but I signaled that I would be fine. We moved as slowly and as quietly as we could. When we reached the landing, it was obvious that someone had been using the place as a shelter. We found empty food wrappers, a sleeping bag and pillow. I wondered if Gerard had also seen this when he had inspected the tower and if so, why he hadn't mentioned it. We decided that there was no reason to climb further and retraced our steps back downstairs, locking the door as we left.

Calm Before the Storm

The trip back to Coopers Mills passed in silence with both Brian and I lost in thought. I sat trying to think about who could be camping out in the light tower. Was it the same person who was lurking around the house? How long had the mysterious visitor been staying there? Had they only just moved in or had they been squatting for some time and why hadn't Gerard mentioned it?

Brian and I arrived at the church where the judging of the quilts was just about to start. We hurried inside and I slipped the hang tag into a clear plastic sheath that Abby had attached to the wooden frame with a clothes pin. Brian went to join his sisters and I took the opportunity to look around the room. There were ten quilts hanging in the room in a sort of u-shape, with Abby's being on one end of the 'u'. All of the entries were beautiful and I wondered how the judge could ever make a decision about which quilt would receive first place.

Suddenly the door opened and three women came in. One of the women announced that the judging would begin and she introduced Laurie Levesque. The introduction caused absolute silence to fall over the room. Abby had said that the judge was nationally renowned and by the reaction of the women in the room, I was beginning to feel like I was in the presence of a celebrity.

Laurie Levesque was about five feet four inches tall with long blonde hair and piercing blue eyes. She had a petite but strong frame and a beautiful figure. She smiled when she was introduced and then motioned to the third woman, who I assumed must be her assistant, and they started moving toward the quilts. The judge moved slowly and methodically, spending quite some time in front of each quilt. Occasionally, she would say something to her assistant who would scribble a note on a pad of paper. At each quilt Laurie not only stood back observing it, but also moved in close, touching the quilt and examining the backing and binding at length. She read each hang tag before moving on to examine the next entry.

While the judge moved around the room, the crowd stood so still and so quietly that I almost forgot they were there. At last she moved in front of Abby's quilt. She stood back looking at it for some time. Eventually she moved in close. She touched the quilt and ran her fingers along the binding as she looked at it. After reading the hang tag, she moved away, centering herself in front of the quilts. She stood there looking at them. She took the note pad from her assistant and seemed to be reading the notes written there.

Just when I thought I would burst from anticipation, she motioned that she was ready to make the awards. She started with honorable mention and worked through third and second place. The winners came forward happily accepting their ribbons from the judge. I was impressed that she took the time to have a few words with each winner, presumably giving them specific feedback on their work.

"First prize goes to Abigail Moorehead for Holly's Storm at Sea," the judge announced.

Between the anticipation, the shock of the judge's words and the thunderous applause in the room, my feet were immobilized. There was a slight commotion in the room as everyone waited for Abby to come forward.

"Can I have Ms. Moorehead please?" the judge called.

"Ms. Levesque," I said moving forward, "I am Abby's

cousin Holly. Abby had an accident this morning and that is why she isn't here. May I accept the award for her?"

The judge studied me for a moment and then handed me the ribbon. More commotion followed in the room as the women who had submitted entries gathered around the judge to thank her and people in the crowd began to talk amongst themselves. The quilts were to be left hanging there throughout the weekend so that the townspeople could enjoy them and have the opportunity to bid to purchase them. Abby's quilt was to be saved for the first prize winner of the festival raffle. As I stood looking at Abby's quilt, Laurie Levesque approached me.

"I am very sorry to hear that your cousin had an accident," she said. "I hope she will be alright. Her work is exceptional. I would have liked to have met her."

"She is one of your biggest fans," I responded. "She was beyond excited to meet you."

"How about if we take this ribbon to her?" Laurie offered.

"Would you…could you really Ms. Levesque?" I asked, startled by the offer.

"I have some time now and if you don't mind driving me, I'd be happy to do it," she answered. "I would really like to meet her."

I excused myself and quickly found Brian, telling him about the judge's offer. He agreed to drive us to the hospital and left to get his truck. Laurie and I waited for him at the door. While we waited, I told her about Abby's car accident, adding that hopefully we would find Abby able to see us. Laurie insisted that we should go and hope for the best.

Brian pulled up and once settled inside the vehicle, we took off. On the way to the hospital I told Laurie about the time I spent helping Abby to make the quilt. The judge listened with great interest and we laughed several times as I told her about some of the funny moments I had trying to play assistant to Abby's masterful skills.

At the hospital, we found my Uncle, my cousins, Miss Molly and Gerard and Casey outside of Abby's room. News of the accident had reached Gerard in town and he had come straight to the hospital expecting to find all of us. They boys had told him as much as they could about the accident and the forgotten hang tag and Gerard knew I would turn up at the hospital eventually. I told the group about Abby's award and introduced Laurie, saying that she had offered to make the award in person. My uncle thanked her for coming to the hospital and told her that it would mean the world to Abby.

We were informed that Abby was resting comfortably and had not sustained any serious injury. My uncle decided that the judge and I should go in while the rest of the group would hang back near the door so that Abby wouldn't be overwhelmed. We opened the door slowly and went in. Abby stirred as we entered. She raised her head from the pillow and smiled at seeing me. She turned her head to look at Laurie and it was obvious from the wide-eyed look of shock on her face that she recognized Laurie. She struggled to sit up and I moved forward to help her, placing her pillow behind her to help hold her up.

"Hello Abigail," Laurie said gently. "I came to bring you your blue ribbon," she continued.

Abby looked from Laurie to me and I smiled, nodding my head in confirmation of what the judge had told her. It was like Abby was star-struck. She smiled and took the ribbon but was speechless. Laurie took it in stride as she told Abby the reasons why she had given her first prize. The judge praised her accuracy of cutting and piecing. She told Abby that her hand binding of the edging was the best she had ever seen. And she said that the visual effect of the design layout and use of colors was stunning.

Abby's face lit up as she took it all in. The scene almost brought tears to my eyes and I noticed that the men folk, although observing quietly from the doorway, were also clearly moved by the scene. Abby managed to say a few words of thanks to Laurie who declared that she must leave in order to catch a flight for her next judging assignment.

Brian offered to take Laurie wherever she needed to go, insisting that I stay with my family. I thanked him sincerely for all that he had done that morning saying I would see him at work the next day and we parted ways. We spent most of the rest of Friday at the hospital with Abby. She would be released on Sunday so we planned to attend church services and then pick her up. We promised her that we would stop by the festival so she could see her quilt and we could check out the mill games and exhibits before bringing her home.

In the early evening, Gerard and I said our goodbyes. I promised Abby that I would visit her Saturday afternoon after I left work at the mill. On the car ride home, Gerard and I discussed the accident and he said that it was obvious that I had been the intended victim, it was just most unfortunate that Abby had been in the car. My mind had not come to that conclusion but as Gerard spoke the words, I knew that he must be right and I knew that despite my fear I must find out who was doing this before someone else I loved was hurt or worse.

Gerard also mentioned that I would need another car but that he would be happy to loan me his car until something could be arranged. He offered to deal with the insurance company for me. As I sat in the passenger seat I glanced over at him realizing just how much he had come to mean to me. I was grateful for his company and his counsel. He was like the father I never had.

At the lighthouse, I made us a light supper and while we ate, I told Gerard all I knew of the day's events. I was surprised at his reaction to the news that we had a mysterious guest staying in the light tower. Instead of being shocked, he said that he had seen the items and assumed that they were from some time ago. And he said that when he and Horace had checked out the tower recently, he must not have latched the door properly when they left the tower. He was sorry that his action had caused me concern and urged me not to give it another thought and to get a good night's sleep.

After doing the dishes, we said goodnight. I lay in bed with Casey beside me. I stroked his fur as I thought about the events of the day. As I did every night before I fell asleep, I thought about Nicholas.

Holly.

There it was again. And yet, it must have been my mind playing tricks on me. Or could someone else be trying to contact me telepathically?

"Nicholas!" I said out loud and then I said it over and over again in my mind but there was no reply.

CHAPTER

Eighteen

Gerard was making breakfast when I awoke on Saturday. He planned to call the insurance company and work on finding me a loaner car, but he readily agreed to let me borrow his car to go to work and visit Abby. With the wave of a hand, I left him and Casey standing at the front door.

At the mill, Brian and I told the girls that I would be looking over accounting entries with him. We took a number of books from the office and among them were the order books from the last two years. We retreated to Brian's office where we poured through the pages of the order books reviewing each order. We found several orders for a Mr. Smith. The address listed was a post office box. Brian said the next step was to pull the actual orders to get the name of the transport company they had used to fulfill the deliveries and see where the lumber had been delivered. He said that I could go back to work with the girls while he pulled the paperwork as it wouldn't look suspicious to anyone if he did it. We decided to meet again when he had all of the documents.

I spent the balance of the morning with the girls in the office and when one o'clock came, the girls gave me some homemade breads and cookies to take to Abby. They said that they hoped I'd find her well. I thanked them, said goodbye and got in the car. As I drove toward the hospital, I thought about what Brian and I had accomplished that morning. I felt that we were on a path to discover the truth.

At the hospital, I found Abby receiving physical therapy in her room. The therapist was helping her to stretch and bend and then they were going to walk around the floor. Abby's prognosis was excellent. She hadn't broken any bones but had just been very badly bruised. They had monitored her for concussion and done a scan of her brain and had declared her safe from any injury there. The therapist said she would give us a few minutes to visit and then come back. Abby was excited to see me and talked of going home the next day. I gave her the gifts from Sandy and Sheila and she was delighted.

"Oh, these are wonderful," Abby exclaimed. "How very thoughtful of the girls."

"I will tell them how much you liked them Abby," I said.

"And how is Brian?" she asked shyly.

"He is doing well. We are busy at the mill," I answered.

"Holly," she continued, "I am very grateful to Brian for his part in my rescue. I know I was in and out of consciousness but I remember him being there with my brothers. I remember words he said to me, telling me that he was there and that I would be okay and to just hang on. And he carried me to the stretcher and I remember feeling safe in his arms."

She stopped, looking at me for my reaction. If she expected shock, she didn't get it. I was smiling warmly because I believed I understood the depth of Brian's feelings for her. And as my own relationship with Brian grew, I felt that a match between the two would be wonderful.

"Abby," I said, "Brian is a fine man. I know you are leaving the hospital tomorrow. Maybe I can arrange for Brian and his sisters to visit you either here before you leave or at the farm. Would you like that?"

"Yes Holly," she answered. "I would really like the chance to thank him for all he did."

"I'm going to go now and let you get back to work," I said. "And I will work on arranging that meeting."

I hugged Abby goodbye. As I was heading out of her room, the therapist was coming back to finish her session. I called to Abby to work hard and she smiled saying that she would.

It was late afternoon when I arrived back at the lighthouse. I found Gerard in the kitchen working on dinner preparations. As I assisted him, I told him of the work that Brian and I had done at the mill and of my visit to Abby. He listened with great interest. Suddenly we heard a car and we left our work to see who our visitor could be.

I was thrilled to see it was Aaron and Nathaniel. They had brought the trellises and hanging swing and wondered if they could install them. They said they had finished work at their farm for the day and figured they would have just enough daylight to make it here and get the work done.

I was thrilled and gave them the go ahead and Gerard invited them to stay and have dinner with us. I called my uncle to tell him the boys had made it there, were going to do their work and then stay to dinner. I also told him about my visit to Abby and how excited she was to be coming home tomorrow. After saying I'd see him at church tomorrow, I hung up.

I had no sooner hung up when the phone rang. It was Sheriff Dineen and he was calling to tell me that my car had been tampered with. As I repeated what he said, Gerard looked up from his work and our eyes met. The sheriff then asked me to explain about the comment I had made at the accident site. I asked him if I could put Gerard on the phone to do the explaining. He agreed and I handed the phone to Gerard and went outside to see how the boys were doing with their work. I found myself overcome at the idea of speaking out loud about the accidents that had thus far taken my family members.

The boys had the swing hung and urged me to try it out. I sat in it watching them assemble the trellises. Behind them the scene of the sun sinking low over the water and down below the horizon line was a peaceful sight. Just as the boys were finishing, Gerard came to the door and called us for dinner.

My cousins washed their hands and offered to set the table. We sat together and enjoyed a delicious dinner. Gerard, a master of sizing up a situation and knowing the remedy, engaged my cousins in conversation about the making of the swing and the trellises and their day at the farm. I knew he did this in an effort to give me a break from all that was worrying me. After dinner, Aaron and Nathaniel insisted on washing the dishes before they left. As I walked them outside and hugged each of them before they got into their truck, I realized that this must be what it was like to have brothers.

Once they left, Gerard announced he was going to make an early evening of it and after saying goodnight, headed up to his room. Instead of heading upstairs, I made myself a cup of hot chocolate, lit a fire in the den and settled into one of the over-sized arm chairs there. Casey laid down on the rug near the fireplace. I cast my mind back over the events of the last couple of weeks.

The accidents, the deaths and all of the conversations. My heart ached for Nicholas and I wished he were with me to help sort it all out. Someone was playing a deadly game but who and why? No matter what angle I thought about, it seemed to me that I always came back to the mill and the Rothchildes. The more I thought about it, the angrier I got at the idea that they could be responsible for hurting the people I loved.

On a sudden whim, I got up and put on my coat, grabbed the keys to Gerard's car from the kitchen counter and headed toward the front door. Casey followed me but I whispered to him that he must stay behind and be on guard. I slipped quietly from the house and into Gerard's car. I started it and moved slowly away from the house. Although I had only been to the Rothchilde cabin once with Nicholas, I felt certain that I could find my way back there.

The road was deserted due to the late hour. About half an hour later found me at the mouth of the long driveway leading to the cabin. I parked the car there and continued on foot in the dark. I had no idea of what I was hoping to prove or find. I couldn't very well ring the doorbell at this hour and start interrogating them.

The house was dark. It popped into my head to try the garage doors. There were three of them. After finding two locked I almost didn't bother to try the third but decided I had better just to be thorough. When I pulled on the door and it opened, I was surprised but I quickly stepped inside and shut the door behind me. I felt along the wall and found what I hoped would be a light switch. I pushed the switch and at once the garage was illuminated in light.

All three of the garage stalls were empty. In the furthest one from me, I saw a retractable hydraulic lift coming up out of the floor. As I looked around the room, I saw all types of tools hanging on the walls and several carts of tools stood around the room. It seemed like an odd set up for a vacation home. Suddenly Max's words came back to me. At the scene of Abby's accident, he had said that he didn't know anything about cars. The Rothchildes had built this cabin so the lift couldn't have belonged to a previous owner. And certainly Margaret was no mechanic. I felt sick with horror realizing what the discovery must mean.

Holly. Come to the mill. Please hurry.

I had an overwhelming feeling of Nicholas. No one but he had ever communicated with me like that. Somehow he must be alive and need my help. I turned off the lights and quietly left the cabin. I made my way as quickly as I could to the car and headed straight for the mill. When I arrived, I could see a dim light inside. There was a boat tied up at the dock and a couple of cars parked in the lot. After parking my car, I cautiously got out and moved toward the door. Just as I reached for the handle, I heard a sound behind me and everything went black.

When I awoke, my head ached. As my eyes adjusted in the darkness, I could hear voices below me. I realized that I was sitting in one of the chairs in a meeting room on the second level of the mill and attempted to get up but I couldn't. I had been tied to the chair.

"Holly?" a voice whispered.

"Brian?" I asked quietly.

"Yes, it's me," he responded.

"What is happening?" I asked. "Where are you?"

"I'm tied in a chair on the other side of the table from you," he started. "It's Max," he continued, "he's gone mad. He called me earlier this evening and said that he had been passing through town and saw lights on here and since it was way past business hours, he thought we should investigate. When I got here I saw a boat tied to the dock and thought that maybe between me and Max we'd finally catch whoever is behind this. Max was near the door, motioning for me to come closer. When I got nearer to him, some men jumped me and I blacked out. When I came to, I was here."

Just then, we could hear someone climbing the stairs. Max came into the room holding a lantern.

"Well, dear sister," he said, "things have rather taken a turn for the worse," he continued, setting the lantern down on the table. "If only Nick had let the taxicab in the street in New York finish you or if only you had been driving your car instead of your cousin and had perished in the accident, I wouldn't have to take extreme measures now. Fate took care of the meddling Nick, one job I didn't have to do myself," he said laughing cruelly.

"Max," Brian interrupted, "you won't get away with this."

"Shut up!" Max commanded roughly. He struggled to regain his composure and then sat down at the table with us. "You have been nothing but a nuisance for years but this is your chance to redeem yourself. When they find the two of you, it's going to look like you killed my dear sister because she discovered you were embezzling from the mill and then you had a tragic accident while trying to escape."

"No one will ever believe that," Brian said defiantly.

"You'd be surprised what people will believe," Max retorted. The room was dark but light from the lantern illuminated his neck and chin. The dim light shining upward on his face gave him a demonic and frightening appearance and I knew that Brian was right. Max was mad.

"Max," I said, finding my voice, "please tell me you aren't responsible for accidents and people dying," I pleaded, although somewhere deep inside I knew what his answer would be.

"Well, since this is just talk among friends," Max said sarcastically, "I will confess that it has all been me. It's not pleasant work but I have learned over the years that if you want something done, and done right, you've got to do it yourself."

"Why Max?" I asked. "You hate me that much?"

"Why?" he exclaimed indignantly. "Your mother had to be punished for ruining our lives. What she did to my father…..how my mother became an empty shell of a person because of their affair…… and then there was you. Bad enough I was constantly in competition with Nick but I was not going to take any back seat to a bastard. Oh, your mother and my father used to talk quite freely at the lighthouse where they thought they were safe. Windows wide open and no one around for miles, or so they thought. There is more than one hollow tree hideout in the woods around your house," he finished laughing.

"How does the mill figure into this?" Brian asked.

"Well, I think if a shrink were to make an educated guess, he'd say that the stress in my life caused me to participate in some unhealthy activities," Max responded disdainfully. "And as a result, I'm heavily indebted to some people. And they are the kind of people that you can't say no to. I was able to siphon off some money from the milling operation to repay some of my debt but when Brian here started to catch on to my creative accounting entries, I was forced to come up with something else to offer besides money."

"I came up with the ingenious plan of using the hollow logs to transport certain items for them for which they are deeply appreciative," he continued. "It worked well for a while until our father started to become suspicious of some of my creative accounting. After he questioned me I knew that there was only one thing I could do. And of course, they had found you and I couldn't allow a relationship between you two to develop. That fool Mike Carter started nosing around and I thought he might be useful so I paid him some money to keep quiet, but in the end, he was too greedy for his own good."

I looked at Brian. I was beginning to sense the desperation of our situation. Suddenly a soft moan came from a darkened corner of the room. Max stood up and took the lantern with him as he went. As light from the lantern illuminated the corner of the room, I saw Margaret Rothchilde sitting tied up in a chair.

Max untied her and pulled her to her feet. She stumbled and he took her by the arm and started toward the door.

As she passed the table she looked towards me and said, "I tried to warn you." At this, Max turned abruptly toward her and she recoiled as though expecting him to strike her. I felt afraid for her and I could feel the anger rising up inside me against Max. I had to come up with a plan.

"I will take care of mother first and then be back for the two of you," Max said as he left, dragging his mother behind him.

"You're absolutely right Brian," I said. "Max is mad. We must get out of here."

As Brian was about to answer, we heard a muffled noise in the hallway. We waited anxiously, looking at the door. Suddenly, Gerard Manning appeared in the doorway on his hands and knees, carrying a flashlight.

"I've brought the cavalry," he whispered as he crawled into the room. He quietly stood up and began to untie the rope that bound Brian's hands. Then Brian came around and untied me.

"Gerard!" I exclaimed, "How did you know we'd be here?"

"My dear," he answered, "we have been monitoring the situation very closely and knew it was time to move in. The sheriff has the place surrounded."

As the three of us poked our heads out of the room, we could see commotion on mill floor below. Lights were being turned on and some men running out of the front door were being stopped by the sheriff's men and Ian. At seeing this, Max abandoned his mother and raced toward the other end of the floor. To our surprise, he jumped onto the conveyor belt and rode up, out and down the water chute into the corral.

We ran out the door by the waterwheel to watch and as we did, we heard a boat engine start up. We saw the boat that had been moored at the dock pull away toward open water. Max had made it past the corralled logs and was swimming in open water toward the boat. Suddenly the boat turned around and headed straight for him. We watched along with the sheriff and his deputies below thinking that the boat would slow down and pick up Max. To our horror, the boat picked up speed and seemed to be heading straight for Max.

"Max!" I yelled, realizing that he was in danger.

I'm already dead. Forget me. I heard it in my head as clear as if he had been standing next to me. Max obviously had the power of telepathy. He must have used it earlier to trick me into thinking Nick was trying to communicate with me. Instead of trying to get out of the boat's path, Max continued to swim toward it. I turned away and buried my face in Gerard's shoulder, unable to watch.

Brian said we had better join the others below. We made our way inside and downstairs where the scene was a busy one. The sheriff's deputies were placing the captured men in cars to be taken away. Cars were leaving the point while others drove onto it. The sheriff explained that the FBI had been notified and would take charge of the investigation as it involved money laundering and the transport of stolen goods across state lines. The FBI would launch a boat to go after the one that had run down Max and would take over the interviews of the transport companies that had delivered the lumber and hollow logs.

As I sat listening to the sheriff, I thought about Nicholas. I wished he could have been there.

Holly…soon, Holly…..

I heard the voice in my head but Max had been killed.

As I sat there wondering who could be communicating with me, the mill door opened and Ian came in, followed by Nicholas. I stood up staring at them.

"Nicholas!" Brian exclaimed, clearly as stunned as I was.

I looked at Gerard who was smiling proudly and not the least bit shocked by Nick's arrival on the scene.

I suddenly felt weak and sank back down onto the chair. Within seconds, Nick crossed the room and knelt down next to me taking me into his arms.

"Oh my God!" I cried, "You're alive!" I sobbed, hugging him tightly.

The scene at the mill wore on long into the wee hours of the morning. Max's body was retrieved and taken charge of by Dr. Thomas who had been called in to move the body to the morgue. Nick had insisted on dealing with this. Gerard had agreed that I should have no part of that and had taken me back inside the mill. I thanked Brian for his bravery and commitment to the mill. I could see that Ian was bursting with pride.

Margaret Rothchilde was badly shaken but agreed to answer the sheriff's questions. She revealed that she had known about her husband and my mother but had feigned ignorance of the affair for years. She had been surprised to learn about me. She had believed that something had been wrong with Max for some time, but she was unable to reach him or control him and she had become afraid of him.

While she disliked me, she had tried to warn me off. She had been made aware of the suspicious accounting entries in the mill's books during Max's oversight of the mill and was afraid that Max had become involved in something bad. She had caught him stuffing hollow logs in the garage at their cabin more than once so she left a hollow log at the lighthouse hoping that I would discover what was going on.

Nicholas said that the strange accounting entries had been noticed and investigated by the company's audit committee. Nick had suspected that Max was up to something but had needed time to let things play out. He did not want Max to realize that things were closing in on him, so Nick decided that if he faked his death, Max would let his guard down. Nick had confided all of this to Gerard who had agreed to help.

Nick had been using the light tower as a shelter where he could watch over me and be nearby if needed. It was he whom I had seen once at the lighthouse in the driveway and at the footbridge at the mill. He had followed me to be nearby if I should need help. And once or twice, against his better judgment, he had reached out telepathically to me by saying my name.

Things concluded at the mill just as the sun was coming up. Nick, Gerard and I decided to head back to the lighthouse for some much needed sleep. We would skip church and meet my Uncle Silas and his boys at the hospital for Abby's release. Brian had overheard the plan and asked if he and his family might join us at the hospital to see Abby. I said yes immediately. At the lighthouse, I called my Uncle to inform him of the change in plans before going to bed. I said nothing about Nick, knowing that was a surprise better left for face to face.

CHAPTER

Nineteen

After several hours of sleep, we rose, showered and ate brunch before heading to the hospital. We arrived at the same time Ian and his family did. Together, we made our way to Abby's room. As we all entered, Nick hung back and remained just outside the door. Inside we found Abby dressed and sitting in a chair with her father and brothers standing around the room.

"Abby, I have a surprise for you," I said.

I held the door open and Nicholas came into the room.

"Nick!" Abby screamed, standing up. Nicholas crossed the room and gave her hug.

There were cries of joy from my uncle and his sons. When the commotion died down, we all found seats and Nick told my uncle and his children of all the latest developments. While Nick spoke, I noticed that Brian had placed himself beside Abby and was holding her hand. Nick spoke of how Brian had been instrumental in helping us to solve all of the mysteries and Abby smiled at Brian with great admiration.

A nurse came in to officially discharge Abby and

we all filed out of the room. In the hallway, my uncle invited everyone back to his farm house to celebrate Abby's homecoming and the end of trouble at the mill.

When Abby was ready, we made our way to our cars and drove to my uncle's farm. It was a cold but beautiful October day. The cars pulled into the farmhouse driveway and the group began to make its way toward the house. Gerard paused and signaled for Nick and me to stop.

"Holly," he asked, "are you finally ready for me to file the necessary paperwork to change your name?"

Before I could answer, Nicholas said, "Thank you but that won't be necessary Gerard. We will be filing a marriage certificate to do that."

Gerard smiled and nodded his head and then started walking toward the house.

"That's okay, isn't it?" Nick asked smiling.

"Yes, that's okay," I said smiling at him and taking his hand as we followed Gerard toward the house.

My storm had passed, leaving true happiness and excitement for the future in its wake.